HOME FOR CHRISTMAS

Clare
Anne
McGrory

Dedication

Home is where the heart is. I dedicate this little tale to my daughter Evelyn, and her brother Sean, and to the rest of my dear family who are all now scattered so far and wide.

Contents

Chapter One

The 6th of December

9am Admiring my figure in the full-length mirror in our hallway, still in my little summer slip-style nightie. Running one hand through my messed-up hair, and pouting demurely, am reminiscent of Faye Dunaway in her classic portrayal of Bonnie Parker. Like her, felt stifled and unfulfilled throughout the entirety of this past year. Although, am not so much keenly awaiting outlaw to sweep me off of my feet and take me on a bank robbing spree to give me a sense of direction in my life, but rather just hoping for a shiny bobble to put on to that engagement ring finger before this year is out.

Have been on a high and almost buzzing with excitement since last night when I overheard my handsome man Ali on the phone discussing the big surprise he was planning for two that had to happen this evening. Had been convinced of his sense of true commitment since he suggested I gave up my room rental arrangement with two other 30-something women of a similar mindset and move in with him to his swanky executive apartment.

What else could it be, if not his cunning plan to propose to me at his posh work Christmas party tonight?

1pm Had showered and pre-washed my hair, for I could barely stand having to make small talk with hairdressers for any longer than was absolutely necessary, let alone stand sitting through the protracted hair washing and conditioning rituals that had become so expensively fashionable to offer in almost any booking above the barber's chop shop. I was now ready to head out to get my hair and make-up done.

Realising how efficient I had been today, I had enough time left for a little impromptu practise proposal engagement speech while Ali was out buying a new shirt for this evening – he mentioned something about the new silk collection at David Jones. If tonight was the night, I wanted to be absolutely ready. Couldn't hurt after all, could it? It wasn't like anyone had ever jinxed themselves by practising saying yes to an intended, was it? I decided not, and got on with it.

Inside my jewellery box I had put my Nanna's engagement ring from much older days, that would be 1946 or so, for safe keeping. She had left it for me specifically in her will, and I was able to collect it when I was up in Brisbane for the funeral in the days after she died. I shuddered for a moment when the thought of what I myself might find myself methodically planning out while waiting on death to reach me in a retirement village, or worse still, old person's home style facility, then reminded myself that for me right now, there could only be lots of good things ahead.

Nanna's ring was perfect for practise, not least of all because it fitted my engagement finger exactly. I had the same ring sizing as Nanna, just as I had the same naturally chestnut hair as her. Although, I had been blonding mine up since I was old enough to get a part-time job and pay for the peroxide out of my own pocket-money. I left it to the professionals to colour it for me these days right enough, so it definitely looked less desperate and less of an attempt to turn into a boy magnet overnight than it perhaps did when I was 16. It was decidedly more Hollywood Siren-esque these days, effortlessly catching the eye of the opposite sex.

2pm Sixteen practise runs at saying yes to Ali's proposal then slipping on Nanna's ring, making sure that looked graceful and poised too, were complete. I think I managed to cover just about everything I could think of in terms of scenarios that could arise, or how he might do it.

Realised then am now about quarter of an hour behind planned schedule to leave the house and make it to hair dressers for styling, so ordering an Uber.

5:30pm Looking in same hallway mirror, appreciating massive transformation from this morning. I look ready for anything, you could stop our ride at the end of a red carpet and I would be good to go.

Sleekest-and-sexiest-undies-I-own-line not visible through satin when I look at my rear – check. Now am totally ready for celebratory sex to seal the intension to marry promise if I am right about his plans tonight, and will also be looking lady-like in the lead up in front of Ali's colleagues.

Saw Ali's bag of purchases from today, not only did he buy the said real silk shirt, but a pair of matching Italian style silk undies!!! When we get home this evening, my night in the bedroom will be hotter than an Italian model-come-WAG of a premier league international football star.

6:30pm Feeling like a true VIP, sporting perfect hair, and wholly appreciating my man Ali when he told me to sit tight as he came around to open the door of my Uber as it pulled up to the hotel entrance where he was chivalrously waiting to escort me inside.

Hotel entrance was flash and sparkly in readiness for Christmas revelries as expected. Could not recall the exact name of the venue we were going to, but it was one of those fancy ones with harbour views and staff whom you could actually expect to notice you and provide you with service as required. That sort of thing.

Getting into the lift ended up being rather squishy when a group of tourists whom I guessed must have been either Canadian or North American from their collective sounds, failed to take the hint that there really wasn't space for all of us to make this trip together at this point. One of them even tread on the soft pointy end of my expensive dress shoes I bought from one of those pricey independent shoe stores in matching satin in a tone close to my dress for this evening. Now it was matching dress and pointed toe shoes with brown smear. Oh, well.

Thankfully, they were getting off about half-way to the top in the hotel room accommodation floors, and we continued up in a more comfortable fashion to dizzying heights towards the flash rooftop bar. I always felt so proud and pleased with myself to be seen out in public with Ali. He always looked impeccable, and anyone could see that nothing on him was ever purchased at bargain prices, or rates within the reach of the common man on the street. His dark complexion, which to many might look as if it were from a travel brochure ad for Greece or Southern Italy, meant that the high fashion menswear from fashion houses over there, as they typically tended to be, suited him perfectly.

8:00pm Had munched through array of high-quality canapes washed down by Champagne, which I think was the real kind, as in it was actually from France. It was definitely not just our local knock off version, lovely as that is too, of course. Patting stomach lightly reassured myself that I wasn't beginning to bloat much at all yet. Perhaps had discovered the secret, should seek out the quality sip of real Champagne in future in the interests of health and waist line.

Next, had sat down for the starter course. They had placed me next to someone who enjoyed a similar position to Ali in their company, he was a fellow executive financial broker for the bank. I discretely copied his, to me at least, peculiar method of consuming the Cream of Broccoli Soup with Yuletide Spice – slowly dip the spoon in at the nearest end of the bowl, then carefully spoon away from oneself until reaching the point of having a reasonably filled soup spoon. After which, precisely bring up to the lips and enjoy carefully, ensuring nothing dribbles down one's cleavage. I saw Ali gesture a wave in my direction while I was becoming quite masterful at that.

I waved back. Then, realising to my shock and horror that I could now feel blood pooling in my rear end when I hadn't even been expecting so much as a bit of spotting by this point in the monthly cycle, I stood up asking to be excused while I nipped off to the little girl's room.

Ali took notice, and he bounced up and over to me planting a kiss on my cheek before I made it to the door. Was pleased, half the room must have seen that. Felt appreciated and secure. Finally.

'What are you doing up and roaming about Meg?' he asked.

'Just going to the little girls' room,' I said.

'Oh, when you get back, I'll show you who I have lined up to spend some with you, after the next course comes out. It's one of the partner's wives, good for networking and all that. So no roaming off after that main course is done. OK?'

Visited the ladies' room swiftly. Only had wingless pads with me, those I carry for emergencies like this one, but they would have to do.

Got back to my seat, made sure to be looking completely calm and in control. Had finally made it. I was a Bonafide executive team wife, worthy of valuable prime dinner chat time with the actual wife of a partner no less.

9pm Mains had just been cleared. Tried to discretely rise in my seat a little to be able to peak over to see if Mrs Forsyth was making her way over yet, or generally looking like she might be about to. Then it happened. Damn it. I could not believe it. I could feel the blood starting to trickle. What horrendous timing.

I was caught in worst dilemma of my new life as the partner, surely soon to be engaged, of top finance executive: if I get up and nip to the little girls' room again, then I risk offending Mrs Forsyth if she comes over here to speak to me in the pre-planned social elevation event for me of the night; while if I stay put, I risk standing up to leave a big bloody darned stain on the seat beneath me and a patch to match at my satin skirt smoothed arse. There was no choice really. I had to make a dash for it now whilst the going was still good.

9:15pm Confirmed that my overall look was still checking out well in the mirrors of the plush ladies' bathroom.

Completed third nervous pedantic check of my rear, well, as far as I was able to see it that was, as I awkwardly tried to glance behind me to the mirror some more. Not a stain in sight, so all clear on that front.

That's when I noticed someone who looked even more out of place than I felt at this posh party. The woman beside me was wearing the cheapest looking cocktail wear that I had ever seen. It was as though she'd taken her kid's doll's clothes and somehow blown them up to be in her dress size. Her unevenly bleached blonde hair looked to be a home done job. And, even though she was certainly well into her late twenties at least, but no more than in her mid-30s, she was projecting an overall impression of going on her late forties due to her badly applied makeup. It was rather caking around the skin and saggy between the lines of any wrinkles she had, while barely covering her pale white skin in between the sporadic streaks of deep sable. To put it plainly, which I don't mind to do in the privacy of my own thoughts, she looked like a common street walker who had just wandered in to the wrong place.

Feeling all the more classy once again. Should in general feel more pleased with myself; am type of woman worthy of a man like Ali who will cherish and honour me.

A cubicle door behind me swung open, and out came another out of place looking woman. Her pretty South-East Asian face also looked similarly over-caked in low quality make-up that was flaking before it even went on.

'You're the lucky ducky again tonight, ain't ya, got that high rollin' Ali bloke again,' said the blonde woman.

Broadest accent I'd heard in a hotel like this in a long time. For a minute my mind took me back to younger days visiting outback Queensland farms on some fashionable farm stay holiday and hearing how the jillaroo girls would call to each other while looking after the herds.

I watched the South-East Asian appearance woman in the mirror while I was fumbling at my hair some more to give me an excuse for lingering. Even just looking at her tiny frame with those narrow shoulders and a body made up of all things dainty, left me feeling a bit self-conscious. It made me feel as though I was more like one of the big heifers on a movie farm set, only waiting on a jillaroo like this one beside me to try to rope me at any minute, while bemoaning my lack of impressive offspring to display to anyone, than I felt like a privileged inner city dwelling lady.

'He is being in mood to spend some tonight I am thinking, will be sure to work him good,' said the petite woman in reply to the blonde one. 'Is usually $400 per private hour session, and he want to offer only portion of rate for quick turnaround tonight. But, I say no, special rate today of $500 per hour as Christmas Party season is busy and I could get other customer easy for full hour at that. You waste my time to hire me only part hour, but not want to pay my hour rate.'

'Smart girl,' said the other one. Then they both trotted out of the bathroom leaving behind them what felt like a cloud of cheap smelling perfume. I almost coughed.

Walking out behind them, I had to pass them in the lifts area to get back into the function room. Heard the blonde one say: 'I knew this was the wrong un, darl. We're meant to be one floor down. They'll all be waiting on us down there, don't want to give 'em any excuse to say they've got there already and we won't be needed for 'em. You know how cheap they all bloody are'.

'Oh, I know,' agreed the smaller woman quickly and hurriedly pressing the down arrow to call the lift. 'Ali money guaranteed for me tonight, don't worry, I make sure of that'.

Hmm, was my first I thought to myself. Hmm. Just Hmm. Then:

She did just say Ali didn't she? And some people down there waiting for them.

Momentarily had what is technically known as a freak out. Reminder to self: not everyone in the world referred to as Ali must be my man Ali! Now, need to get back to being graceful, alluring, yet not overtly sexual, respectable partner that any 40 something successful man like my Ali can be proud of. Oh, and suitably grovel to impress Mrs Forsyth.

Entering in through the widely opened doors to the function room, it hits me again. It's that sinking feeling. My man Ali is not in sight. Where the bloody hell could I be? Now their bad language is rubbing off on me, but keeping it in my head only, so all good.

A few steps towards my table, then nope, I just cannot do this. Something does not feel right at all. And Ali is not in room.

It'll only take 5 minutes. I reassured myself. *Mrs Forsyth won't die off or anything waiting on me just for that much longer.*

9:40pm Gently, but firmly, pressing on the down button calling a lift. Best to get the checking out of this situation over and done with. Will prove fears unfounded.

9:41pm Slightly banging impatiently on the lift button now, but trying not to get noticed doing so.

9:42pm Finally. Step off one floor below. Can see immediately that it is a residential floor. This is not the function area, nor does there appear to be any communal amenity areas located on this level either.

I hear a door swing closed with an over loud of a bang to one end of the corridor and follow that sound. Then as I move closer, start to hear, 'Oh, yes, you Ali, you must join us now'.

Pausing for a moment, I notice a cuff link that I recognise apparently dropped unnoticed on the ground outside of a door. All inside were obviously too excited to keep the noise down too.

Wonder if I should just call an Uber now and head home.

But in a way, it felt rather like hearing there's a car crash up ahead on the drive home for Christmas. You know that if you look you might spend the rest of your life waking from haunted dreams of seeing dead or dying bloodied faces before you, and yet, for some strange reason, you just can't go past it. You have to stop to have a right proper look. And similarly, so did I right now.

Deep breath. I can do this. Can't stand in the corridor listening to squeals and giggles of delight with a single tear forming in the corner of my eye as I look down at one of those cufflinks I got him as a Valentine's gift earlier this year forever.

One good hard push, and the door is opening so that I am already on my way in to see for myself what is actually going on before I can even register it.

No need to open any door to see into the bathing area my man Ali is in. The spa suite rooms such as this one on the upper levels with views out to the bay have a voyeur compatible set up anyway. I see that there is nothing but Japanese inspired transparent toughened glass sliders separating the soapy bubble hub from the rest of the suite.

They hadn't felt the need to draw those closed either. And when I say 'they', by that I mean my man Ali, and not just one, but two petite women of South East appearance minus their clothing by now and already lathering each other up while he crawls on the floor making an appearance that to my mind is like some strange cross between a lurching dog and a sad, past his prime, exotic male revue dancer. The silky boxers were still on.

Then he had the gall to say: 'Meg, this really isn't what you think it is.'

I could hear the tail end of that sentence from him, my now ex-man Ali. From that point, I just bolted out of that room and then made my way down towards the open street via the emergency stairwell.

Not wise to stop to wait on a lift in case useless now ex-man came out to attempt mediation in his silky underpants hanging over fading erection for whole world to see.

10:00pm Legs dangling from a park bench, I saw one of the Sydney Harbour Ferries roll in to the quay at Barangaroo. Watched scores of happy looking people embark and disembark - check. Thought of what it might feel like if I just leapt up and into that dark water of the harbour right now – check. Thought of how little anyone around me at this moment would actually care – check.

Realised reassuringly that I was far enough away from the hotel Ali was at so as not to be easily found by him if on the off chance he did decide to roam the streets trying to find me, but not so far away as to be lost.

10:15pm Incontrollable sobbing had settled by this point. Made phone call to old house-mates Jacquie and Amy telling them I needed a couch for the night, and would they, and whoever replaced me in what I thought was the end days of my old tragically single for far too long life, mind if I come by tonight?

10:45pm Amy arrives and comes jogging over to where I'm still seated on the bench feeling the chill of the sea breeze. I notice it is starting to make me overly cold, even on this summer's evening. Perhaps I was in shock. After leaving that place packed full of those oh so very important seeming people dressed up to the nines. Amy looked so very, well – ordinary. There was something comforting about that simple fact alone.

'Jacquie's parked just around that building,' she said to me. 'Come quick, don't want to get a ticket or anything, Goodness knows the Christmas budget is tight enough as it is this year, chez us lot.'

Chapter Two

The 7th of December

2:34pm in the afternoon Am just now this moment awake. Everything feels rather strange. Looking at my hands, wiggling my fingers and toes a bit. Now absolutely reassured that, no, this is not a dream.

Good thing about my having access to Amy's medicine cupboard last night. Was the first time I had taken Xanax in my life, yet two little tablets and 20 minutes later I was sleeping like a baby, even after my whole world just fell apart.

Bad thing about my access to Amy's medicine cupboard last night: I feel comfortably numb, like I could be better occupied right now if I were doing some air guitar and gently swaying than thinking about anything, even after my whole world just fell apart.

'Oh, I thought I heard you rumbling over there,' said Jacquie from behind her coffee mug in the corner kitchen alcove as I stumbled in. 'You made it. He screwed you over, proved he's just another scumbag, but you have survived.'

Like, say what? Now "I will survive" is streaming through my head.

Actually did then take a pause and just sway some. Feeling the air around me. Centring.

Then, noticed Amy looking a little concerned.

'Does anyone ever actually check if you give your script only meds to other people?' she was saying to Jacquie.

7.00pm Looking at what might become my third bread roll of this dinner. Sorry, but simply must have it too. There's no other way, I cannot see what could be an alternative option for me right now.

I still live in hope that one day I will join those lucky ones who find they can't eat when stressed and depressed. *Why does it have to be the exact opposite for me?*

As it was, I had instead been sitting making a head start on the amazing feat of gaining even more extra pounds to haul about the place whilst continually nodding whenever I thought that it was expected of me, because in truth, I wasn't taking in a word of what anyone was saying. It seemed to be in general, supportive however, and that's what counts.

The 8th of December

9:05am Through groggy slowly opening eyes, saw that I had managed to rise nearer to a normal hour this morning. Too late to say I was on the mend, but even after a moment of fleeting recall of what my new single situation in the lead up to Christmas really was, I knew I could get through this.

For some reason my late Gran popped into my head. 'You're a tough cookie you are!' She would always say to me.

I suppose I am. But I wish I didn't have to be.

Why couldn't someone just, well, love, ... me?

9:15am Received a reply from boss to my email telling her that I was unable to come into work today due to a personal matter. She said she was fine with it. But they always say that, don't they? You find out if your boss is really fine with things when you still have a job six months later is my own experience.

But you know, for the very first time in my entire life, I actually did not care.

Afterall, what did I really have here anyway? All these dedicated years as a professional working women doing the daily office thing in Syndey, and what did I really have to show for it all?

I could call myself team leader level now. But so what? Did I have any real estate here that I owned? No. Did I have any true love partner I knew would be with me until the first of us should depart? No. How many times had I even gone to the lovely nearby beaches all around us to take a dip on a hot day in the last year? None. Unbelievable.

I realised at that point, that somewhere along the way to this stage in my life, I had utterly lost track of everything I had actually aspired towards in my younger years.

Then Gran popped into my head again, and Grandad too. By the time they were in their thirties like me, they'd already had Mum, and Uncle Brian. They knew they'd always have each other. And they were right. They did.

Next thing that popped into head was the phone call I got several months ago from my cousin up in Queensland who gave me the news that Gran had passed away in a nursing home. She told me that staff said the night before she went she had dreamt about Grandad. 'He was up there waiting on her,' she said. Tears started to well up in my eyes.

Suddenly, I was hit with a crushing almost unbearable feeling once again: *no-one will ever love me the way I want to be loved, and it's just not fair.*

That was when the crying began.

10:20am Realised I was still crying. Looked in the mirror and saw how swollen and puffy my lips and eyelids were ... at which point a huge *wail* just came flowing out of me.

Aforementioned wail brought Amy rushing in to my room looking terrified.

'What's happening, are you ok?' she was asking.

I felt myself already having automatically begun blurting out the standard 'oh, I'm alright,' reply, when I realised that I really wasn't. I had been utterly wrong earlier. I wasn't feeling so much of a tough cookie, as a sad, melting, gooey, doughy, mess, that had been left out in the heat too long or something, such that no-one would touch it with a barge pole.

The sudden ordinary thought of how I would have to be in work tomorrow, facing the day as usual, made me feel sort of woozy.

Noticing how I was actually starting to sway on my feet, Amy promptly rushed over to steady me with a hand.

I let out a weak 'Thank you,' which somewhat resembled a bleat from a lamb, then sunk down into the bed.

'You know what you have do?' said Amy looking perplexed. 'You have to call up and get an appointment with your GP. You need some time to recover from this one. Being honest, you really don't look so good right now, it's like all the blood has drained down to your toes or something, you are so pale looking.'

Urrrgh. I groaned.

I knew she was right though.

Former housemates truly were the best. This was the closest thing to having a sick and home from school with supportive Mum Day that one could have as a grown up.

My own mother had passed away when I was still quite young of course. Then Dad about five years ago, having drunk himself to death, not that I wasn't still sad and sympathetic about it though, of course.

I still had a few years of fond memories of both of them.

4:20pm Still donning sunglasses even whilst inside, I sat blankly staring at my GP while she too was very kind and sympathetic. I hadn't been expecting quite so much concern over my current state of mind to be honest.

I was stunned though at what she said next: 'you need to take until the end of the month off as stress leave, and I would recommend you see a counsellor too. You can even do that via telehealth these days, which is often handy if you might like to go say have some rest by the beach or with family somewhere. I'm writing you a medical certificate that expires on the 1st of January 2026.'

It took a while to sink in.

On one hand, I knew I probably needed it, especially if a doctor thought so, they know best of course. I knew I deserved it too. I had worked so hard for so long. Yet, I felt guilty. I had joined two rather sad sack grouping categories among the Australian statistics in these past few days: I was both part of the tragically single and horribly betrayed by partner crowd **and** the not coping at all psychologically and badly needing time out from life to recover camp. All the while of course, I was feeling it was somehow all my own silly fault. I think that feeling must capture the one overarching category that's commonly underlying all of the above, however.

7:30pm After the three of us tucked away at dinner, we sat enjoying some wine, as we had increasingly come to do just about every night of the week.

'I can't believe you got such a great sickie note from your doctor Meg,' said Jacquie, who had been as stunned as I had been when I got it when I first told her about it.

'I know, but it occurred to me, that I'm not even sure I have that much stacked up on paid sick days at work,' I said. That was the first time that thought had actually occurred to me, my grip on the practicalities of life obviously slowly returning to me.

'But you know what,' said Amy most insightfully: 'What the bloody hell does it even matter?'

I paused for a moment doing some quick calculations in my head, then said 'You're right.'

'I know I am,' she went on. 'Say you have a couple of weeks, and then you have to spend some savings for the next couple of weeks before you go back to work, well, it's not like you have any rent to pay since you had just been living with Ali. He's the only one legally responsible for the rent on your old place now.'

'True that,' agreed Jacquie. 'You can certainly afford this well-needed break. Some people would see this as like a once-in-a-lifetime opportunity.'

'When you put it like that. I suppose it is a bit of a silver lining to this absolutely rotten start to the Christmas season.'

'Have you had a think yet about what you want to do for the coming weeks?' asked Amy. 'Because if you don't plan some things, the time will pass so quickly. You could go somewhere nice out of town for a while, or back home to Brisbane.'

'To swelter in the sub-tropical heat that is classic December weather up there while us poor sods work away down here,' Jacquie added, most descriptively.

'It has been a while since I went back up there,' I said. 'I didn't even manage to get up there for Gran's funeral back in June. That was since I didn't really want to skip out on that weekend away that Ali had planned for us to go ski over in Christchurch for a few days which, if you remember, happened to be when she passed away. Ali had convinced me to stay on the ski holiday when I got the news. I didn't enjoy the rest of that trip anyway of course, because I just felt so bloody guilty about it all.'

'Your Gran did so much mothering for you, and that makes it all the harder to lose her,' Jacquie added in her usual understanding way.

'Yes, she really did step up and step in quite a bit for us when Mum died. Just when she should have been enjoying being an empty-nester Grannie,' I recalled becoming quite wistful, then a bit melancholy. I didn't want to fall into that sinking feeling again though, so I tried to bring my mind back to something constructive.

'You know what I could maybe focus on during this time?' I said excitedly having just enjoyed a moment of renewed inspiration and drive. 'Finally working towards a longer-term plan that for that old first home of Gran and Grandad that she left behind in trust for me and my cousin. I forgot they even had that property supplementing their income in retirement for years, and since the lawyers transferred the trust over to us, I have just been collecting the rent without so much as a second thought about what's going on in that little old place.'

'That's a great idea Meg,' said Amy.

'I'll call up tomorrow and ask the estate agent what's been happening with it, then I'll see if I can get a reasonably priced airfare up to Brisbane,' I decided.

'I hate to mention this, because it's not a pleasant thing to deal with, but when are you going to go collect your things from your and Ali's old place?' added Jacquie, ever practical.

'Oh, God. I had somehow forgotten about that one. Any volunteers to sneak over there with me around lunchtime tomorrow? He never, ever comes back during the day on a week day when he's at work, and I just don't want to see him. I don't want to see his face ever again so long as I live in fact.'

'Fair enough,' said Amy.

'I can volunteer for the lunchtime session tomorrow,' said Jacquie helpfully. 'We can use our car. You just need to come pick me up at the office, and I'll come with you then to help you pack your things up. I kept some old moving boxes from our last move, luckily. I think the plan should be to just quickly chuck all you can in to your suitcase, then into the boxes, pack up the car, then get out of there, and worry about the rest when you get back here.'

'Sounds like a plan,' I said, trying to brave up for tomorrow. I knew that he never comes home through the day and so I shouldn't be nervous about it, but I still couldn't help but to struggle with that old *what if* thought. I really didn't know if I could even handle it if I saw him. What if I had some kind of meltdown and tried to take a swing at him, or slap him in the face, or what if I outright collapsed under the pressure? Afterall, I was feeling a tension headache rising right now at the mere thought of it.

When I thought about Ali at this point, the only mental image I would get flashing up before my eyes was the gaze my eyes had instantly been drawn to in those new silky boxers he had just bought himself, and which he'd happily stripped down to. It had been obscured only by the sexy lingerie-clad bodies of the two women 'servicing' him down there, and everywhere, or however they put it these days.

Enough. He is out of my life.

The 9ᵗʰ of December

12:30pm It was lunchtime for all poor sods trapped in their offices. And Jacquie and I had just come out of the lift on the floor of my old apartment. I held the lift door open with one arm and peeked out to make sure the corridor was clear before exiting causing Jacquie to walk into my rear having anticipated I would get out of the lift like a normal person. Afterall, it wasn't like there would be anywhere to run to at this point if Ali had happened to be standing in the corridor or something.

I listened at the door just to reassure myself that there were no sounds that might indicate anyone was inside before opening it up.

Everything looked just as it was on Saturday evening before we left for that party. I don't know why that should have felt surprising, however.

There were no empty drink bottles littering the room. Nor well tossed and turned in bedsheets discarded on the couch. Nor in fact a single thing at all that would have suggested Ali was having anything resembling a hard time, a troubled conscious, or feeling out of sorts since I left.

It was like absolutely nothing had happened.

'He had no heart,' I suddenly blurted out, staring at the cold reality of it all, and realising that this was my last glimpse of that couple life I had been so emotionally invested in since the start of this year. It was just moving into my past now. On to the next chapter of the rather ordinary life of me, Megan Russell.

'A man with no heart, is like a gaping black-hole encapsulated in an overly restrictive outer shell, meaning that only one future can possibly arrive - one that sees you sucked into that abyss as all that makes you feel grounded, and all things that you hold dear, are whisked away from you forever.'

I just stared at her for a moment. 'That's deep Jacquie.'

She hugged me, then snapped us both back to the here and now with: 'Right, let's get packing.'

12:55pm After trundling my only overly filled only suitcase, my vanity carryon bag, and a couple of those packing boxes filled with my belongings down to the car park, I took one last look at the place, and let out a long doleful sigh.

'Come on,' said Jacquie. 'It's just the car park. He's really not even worth another moment of your thoughts or time. Let's get out of here. So long Ali.'

Chapter Three

The 12th of December

2:35pm Walked out of arrivals in the Domestic Terminal of Brisbane Airport, and the wall of heat instantly hit me. I could feel it enveloping me like a hot, thick, sticky, and moist invisible blanket.

How on earth did I put up with this as a child? We didn't even have air conditioning in our school rooms back in those days, for God's sake!

Then I noticed how the bright blinding sunlight was twinkling in one of the Christmas adornments outside, and thought, *this is just so typically Christmas in Queensland.*

I am home for Christmas!

2:45pm I sat wilting on the platform awaiting the arrival of the *Airtrain*. I was so tempted to just walk back over to the terminal and grab a taxi, or call an Uber - that way I could pre-order 'extra-cool' as the ambience choice before it arrived and have something to look forward to. But really must be sensible with my money.

The heat was already making me feel drained and weak. I was not used to this anymore. The the humdrum memory of the reality of my situation set in though. I didn't want to eat through all my spare cash in the first couple of weeks, this month was a time to go back to basics for a while. *This would be character building and do me good*, I reassured myself. Besides, cousin Tilly, the trendy thing, was living on one of those swanky new apartments right in the CBD. I would have to get used to getting around on my two legs again to make the most out of that advantageous residential situation in the new more bustling city centre of Brisbane.

When I was just a kid growing up in Brisbane, in spite of the sizeable population and massive sprawl of the city, I remember how the CBD was pretty quiet outside of week day office hours. While some of the office buildings stood tall over the place, there weren't all of these new residential and hotel towers invading the city centre yet.

I found it all a bit strange and disconcerting really, because each time I came up to visit in recent years, there seemed to be either another new building up touching the sky already, or one in progress and reaching towards it. The development was happening quicker than I felt I could adjust to.

At first, most people assumed it would primarily be overseas investors and foreign students attracted to living in those new builds. After all, it might feel more like home to them if they've just come over here from say Hong Kong, or Seoul, or some other big Asian metropolis. They have, for as long as they've known them, been full of high-rise buildings, and with streets bursting at the seams day and night. But surprisingly, a number of aging baby boomers who had been born and bred in Queensland also seemed to have decided it would better suit them to move into these new fancy modern towers too. After all, most of them had spent the best decades of their lives mowing lawns on a Sunday, even in the blistering heat, scooping leaves out of pools, painting flaking fences, window sills, and endless awnings as were so typical on the classic Brisbane home, while simultaneously raising a brood of often ungrateful children. I'm sure there must have been something quite liberating for a lot of those types to just wave goodbye and move into something low maintenance where they still had a communal pool or BBQ area should they feel like using it.

The realisation hit me though, that as some of the people in that situation were already moving on having completed that part of their lives involving raising children in the standard Australian family home, I hadn't even got anywhere near starting such a life yet.

Shoved that thought to the back of my mind as fast as it had popped into the forefront of it because it was both scary and a little depressing.

Something I liked about the new busier central Brisbane though, was the new array of eateries that had sprung up everywhere from right in the middle of the central shopping mall, to little out of sight back allies that used to be largely ignored by Brisbanites looking to set up a business. There really was something for everyone in the city centre now, and you didn't have to be home and getting ready for bed by 9:30pm anymore because absolutely everything was closed by 9pm back in those days. That was truly how it was not so very long ago at all.

Brisbane was truly turning into more of a typical city of the world now. But as someone who had the privilege of knowing it when it was more like a big country town that called itself a city, and behaved as such at times, I felt sad that those days were truly gone now.

3:30pm Gracious me. Had made it to Roma Street Station, and it was just far too busy, not to mention confusing. There were so many exits, and poor attempts at temporary type signage. It seemed this place was also undergoing construction or renovations, as just about everywhere here seemed to be lately.

This was a moment during which I missed the old Brisbane again. In the days of my youth, I'd be expecting to walk out to a relative waiting out front in their car to pick me up ... but, in this transition towards a new type of lifestyle in Brisbane, I don't think cousin Tilly even owns a car!

4:30pm Had walked from the station to cousin Tilly's house, being green, fit and all that. It was not like I didn't travel on foot around Sydney fairly often, but the difference was, that when you venture out in the summer heat up here in Brisbane, within the first three steps you're already covered in a light mist that you soon feel start to settle all over your body, even the skin on your face. Further, by the time you reach your destination, if it's anything more than a ten-minute walk, the average person has developed some interesting sweat patches, most notably on the back, under the arms, and in the under the boob area, as I always tend to call it. That last spot, last, but by no means least, while affecting females the most, can often be seen on men too.

Realised at this point, that by the time I had found my way out of the station, got lost a couple of times enroute to the apartments, and waited what seemed like a mini eternity at each and every pedestrian crossing I reached – that was one thing in Brisbane that just hadn't changed, even since they had installed numerous automated buttons removing the need to bang hard on a circular piece of metal at every intersection. It took even longer getting from the station to the apartment than it had to come all the way into the city from the airport. So much for the modern newfangled European inspired green, cosmo, convenient (supposedly), new inner city Brisbanite's lifestyle.

4:35pm Cousin Tilly standing in her door to greet me as I arrived up onto her floor was such a welcome sight. When we gave each other a big hug, all the most wonderful memories of years long ago came back in one big all-encompassing wave of happy emotion. From shadows of how we grew up together playing in the yard, or snuck out at night as teenagers to meet our first young high school crushes, then on to going out to hotels for drinks on a Friday night in our student days, those were the best days of all, I think.

'You're looking great!' I said to her. *So much more fashionable than me*, I was thinking. But she was in the arts world, with her job as a lighting technician for the stage and all that. It's expected in their world to keep up with the trends. People like me spend way too much time queueing up for lattes and catching trains from the suburbs to have time for it all.

'You are too,' she said to me so encouragingly. 'And while you're up here, we should take you out for a make-over or something. You still have the 90s look hair, and don't get me wrong, it suits you still, but you should try something more modern like mine. You've got some time all to yourself just to chill and take care of yourself, so why not? If you don't like it, you can always grow it out again.'

My hair ... it's like a comfort blanket! Every day when I get up and see myself in the mirror, it looks like it has done for the last 15 years, and that helps me pretend that the hands of time haven't marched on so very much in the mean time at all.

'Maybe,' I said. 'But hey, let's go inside. I need some cold water; I am sweating so much.'

The 13th of December

7:00am Something about the brightness of the Brisbane sun, combined with the fact that Queenslanders still just refuse to adopt daylight savings time, had me up earlier than usual for a not at work day.

Feeling healthier already.

8:00am At Southbank, Brisbane's most touristy spot, having breakfast by the river. This is the life.

'So, the house then, let's start going over some of the practical issues and think about what we might want to do, if anything,' began Tilly.

'Well, first of all,' she continued, in between finishing off the last piece of her eggs Benedict brekkie, 'the rent currently, just as it all is, is absolutely brilliant. I mean, $750 a week is pretty decent, some agents fees of course, but even when split between the two of us, I've found that amazing in the last few months. It's just so liberating. I am happy staying in the job I love now. I'm not feeling pressure to think about getting myself higher pay simply to make ends meet any more. I maybe would have to move somewhere else to get that, or even leave the theatre world altogether' for it, which would be devastating.'

'When you say just as it all is, what do you mean?'

'I mean given that the place is quite run down.'

I hadn't actually seen the place in years, and even then, it was just quick a view out of the car window. I caught a glimpse as we were passing the street the time when Dad took me to a University of Queensland open day. I remember he said, 'Oh, your Grandparents own that little house there. It's their rental property now. They moved into it in the 1940s right after they got married, and at the end of World War 2. Special place for them that was, their first home, and where they first started raising your Mum and uncle.'

I had a vague recollection of looking out of the window and seeing a pretty standard Queensland style home, maybe built around the 1940s. I realised though it's like a mansion of sorts compared to modern housing situations, especially around there, where real estate became such a hot commodity long ago. That was long before it started happening everywhere, due to the proximity to the university.

It was rather strange now in fact, to think of people like my Grandparents, with my Grandad just working a blue-collar job on the university staff, being able to afford a four-bedroom house with a yard within walking distance of his workplace. Professors even should be so lucky nowadays.

'I actually hadn't even given any thought to the idea of whether we would ever renovate that place, I mean, I don't really have a lot of savings right now,' I said coming back to some practical considerations.

'The bottom-line or cold hard reality is, we would have to take a loan out on the equity in the property if we wanted to do something like that, but that's a big step. We'd really have to think carefully about it,' said Tilly.

'True,' I agreed. 'And also, we'd run the risk that if the budget blew out, as I read it often does these days when you try to build or renovate in Brisbane, what with the inflated workmen's rates, materials price hikes, and scarcity of skilled tradies, then some of them even raising their quotes as they go along and after they've started, that we might have to sell our project when completed to pay off the bills. While that type of reno gone wrong might lead to a tidy nest egg for us to split in any case, it would mean the end of our guaranteed steady and rationed out to us income that we could just stick with having for the foreseeable future.'

'There could be some other factors though, that we haven't really been thinking about yet.'

'Like what?' I asked her.

'Well, with the recent land grabs and developments in this city, there's been growing pressure to remove old houses like our one which are currently sitting among unit blocks already by this stage, and then have the developers coming in and putting up more apartments in their place. The way they see it, they could have a whole tower full of people in that one spot where we currently have 3 or 4 students lounging around with their own front and back door and bit of grass around them.'

'But,' I gasped out, 'it's an old-style typical Queensland post-war home, it's part of the historical character of the suburb, or what's left of it. It's unthinkable, surely.'

'Well, it's not really unthinkable Meg, is it? I mean, don't you remember how many more wooden houses used to be around this city when we were growing up, compared to now? They've demolished with council approval, or just quietly burnt down overnight, much older and more historic residences than that one too. Some old Queenslanders have long been gotten rid of over the years. It's really just a few elite old style family suburbs that still get to live that type of lifestyle here now. And our house isn't on the heritage list or anything, so while it may be old, it's not legally protected really.'

My heart had sunk a little. *The age-old conundrum of the price of progress.*

'You know, right now there are no tenants in it,' said Tilly. 'I've been a bit surprised in fact given where it is. Usually, we get a new one moving in as soon as one moves out.'

'You don't think the estate agents are screwing us over or something, do you? You know what their reputation is like here.'

'Could be,' said Tilly. 'And with so much developer interest around here, them looking to swoop in and make a quick buck, maybe they're trying to get us out of the rental market so they can convince us to make a sale. They might have bigger plans in mind than our little rental business, ones that make them and their friends even more money. Which is why I was thinking, given you saying you wanted to take some time to actually look at the house etc while you are up here, why don't you check that theory out?'

'I'd like to,' I said. 'Given it's not tenanted right now, I assume I am allowed to just take the key and go over there any time I feel like it, right?'

'Yes.'

'And you have a key, don't you?' I asked Tilly. 'I have never seen a copy of any keys, since the estate agents were just carrying on with managing it and all that.'

'Yes, I have one at home. The estate agents have a spare set too of course, and the set they give out to the tenants. I'll call them and ask them just to be sure to let us know if they are lining up anyone to move in, or planning an open house or something so you can avoid clashing with them on your visits to the place. But, if you're there, and they show up with one or two people for a private inspection or something, it's not really that big of a deal, I shouldn't imagine. Just make sure it's always kept fairly tidy whenever you're there. Not that it's exactly like a show home anyway, given it's been a student pad for decades by this point.'

'Sure.'

Chapter Four

The 14th of December

6:45am Already onboard the city cat and almost at St Lucia. Feeling the breeze from the river rapidly rush at my face on this section where they pick up some speed was exhilarating.

Glad I headed out early to beat the heat because it's gotten pretty warm already.

7:15am Have arrived outside the gate of what is truly half my own little property. Feels strange frankly. Pushing the wooden gate inwards made it creak so that I was frightened to be too forceful in case I broke it. I wondered if it was in fact an original gate from circa 1946, or back when this was a new build in other words. I found that thought mind boggling. So, I carried on without much more fussing up to the entrance door to make my way inside.

The quintessential Queensland post-war home this was.

I allowed myself a moment to look past what I guess were early 1990s style furnishings that would only be tolerated by the likes of poor and dollar scrimping students these days. I tried to imagine what this would have looked like back in 1946 or 1947 when my newly wed Nanna and Grandad would have been coming in here to stake their claim in their own little starter family home.

I imagined Grandad lifting Nanna up, she would have been much slimmer back then, and carrying her over the threshold. He really was a stickler for traditions that man, and she loved that about him.

I glanced over to the compact kitchen area that nowadays sported a corner wrapping proper wall hugging kitchen bench top with its standard in-built sink. Then I tried to visualise it with an old standalone oven, sink on tall stilts, and a separate table top style cutting and chopping area. How excited they would have been about it all though back in the day. Imagining it all as it was brought an immense sense of elation in to me at this present moment.

I breathed in and held my breath to savour the feeling. Then, as I slowly let the air out of me, all of a sudden it was accompanied by an even stronger feeling of emptiness and disappointment than I had felt when I first caught Ali cheating. *Would I ever find someone who wanted to share their life with me like that and who I could feel sure wasn't lying to me in every other sentence they uttered?*

Although Nanna and Grandad would have been totally thrilled with it anyway, this house would have been considered just a cheapie back then. Nothing more than just a standard place for ordinary enough type folk setting up home. Ironically, with the massive increase in the land value in this suburb, coupled with the natural passage of time making the old house look rather quaint in comparison to the newer more sterile brick style homes, it was now a truly enviable asset, and not at all within the reach of ordinary type folk working ordinary type jobs with no family money behind them.

My, how things change.

8am Back out to the front veranda, and I stood for a moment just feeling the ever warmer and moistening air rising up and tickling my fingertips as the temperature of this hot Brisbane summer's morning quickly stretched into full blast as the clock ticked on.

I thought about walking back out to the gate to take a look up and down the street, but realised I hadn't brought a hat, so I'd be feeling the tip of my head burning if I ventured out of the shade. Too used to cooler Sydney with plenty of sky scraper building shade nowadays, it's got me forgetting my good habits I was raised with here: always stand in the shade where possible, even if it's just the long skinny shadow cast by a traffic crossing lights pole; always wear a hat with a big wide brim; and slip, slap, slop on that sunscreen of course.

But then, the neighbourhood world of this little old house suddenly started coming in to find me and to see me.

'Oh, hello,' a round shiny faced and plump young man was saying whilst waving at me so vigorously. I can vaguely recall the time when I used to have that much energy myself. It was rather nice though, to see a smiling face from a well-meaning stranger that is.

'Hi there,' I called out back to him.

He just opened the gate and began walking in. Friendly indeed.

'Are you the new tenant in here then?' he asked.

'Oh, nope, not me,' I answered him. 'I'm afraid I'm just one of the crusty old landlords.'

His blank face and wide-eyed stare showed just how much I had truly shocked him for a moment or two, and made me realise just how flat my joke had fallen.

'You're the actual owner then,' he said recovering his stride in a moment or two. 'I had always wondered who owns this place, but I actually expected you to be quite a bit older. Are you moving into the place now then?'

'No, just taking a look around, I don't live in Brissie these days.'

'Well, my name's Matt, and I live next door.'

'Nice to meet you Matt,' I said. 'Do you work around here?'

'I study mainly, but work a little too. I'm a mature student at UQ, studying physio.'

'Good career,' I said encouragingly.

'So, if you don't live around here these days, where do you live?'

'Sydney,' I said, realising yet again in that moment that it really didn't feel like home to me back down there at all. I had nothing in the place, except a few boxes of my worldly possessions over-staying their welcome in my friends' house. *This type of negative thinking is what I am meant to be distracting myself from however.*

'Like it down there?'

'There's good and bad things about,' I said vaguely. 'Like any place.'

'Well, glad to see you here, and enjoy your stay in Brisbane.'

10am Realised what I am totally missing is some good photos of this old house. *Our* old house. It was a good feeling actually, even if a bit surreal, to realise I actually own 50% of something substantial. Maybe if I had saved up for it and paid the mortgage bit by bit over the years of hard slog, it would all have felt more tangible. To just have this handed to me was something more to actually take in.

10:15am Headed out on to the pavement to get some better photographs from a wider angle of the front of the little wooden home.

Standing on the nature strip just in front of the fence, I took a moment to actually look at the place properly myself. The casement style all wooden frame windows seemed to peep out to the world like private little eyes. The weatherboards that made up the outer walls were still in good condition. The paint was starting to look a bit shabby in the odd spot or two, some peel was starting, particularly on the side facing the road, but overall, it was clear to see it had always been well maintained, up until this point at least. Thank goodness none of the wood had ever been allowed to rot.

As I was starting to recall some more things I must've learned along the way growing up, I added a reminder to my phone to check with Tilly that we definitely are all up to date with things like regular termite checks and barrier sprays being arranged.

10:27am Now had a good collection of nice photographs of the front side, but would be quite perfect if I could just step a little further out to get an even wider shot.

Schools in this suburb were now on holidays for Christmas, as were the university students, so the road was fairly quiet. There was a nice wide bicycle lane running along side the pavement. *Ideal.*

Stepping back a little on to that, after carefully checking it was clear, I quickly took another great snap on my phone camera. But when back on the pavement I noticed suddenly that half of my thumb was in the way. *Quickly redo that one then.*

Just as I stepped back, I realised half-way that I hadn't actually checked it was clear this time.

'Shit!' I heard in the loudest voice.

I hopped back up on to the pavement, looked around and saw a fit looking Lycra-clad cyclist just beyond me lying on the ground flailing, his bike wheels still spinning as the frame lay on his side. He was on the nature strip by the pavement, but his bike was straddling that and the bike lane on the road.

Oh God, he's bleeding.

'Are you alright?' I said rushing over to him. 'I'm so sorry, I just didn't see you there, I didn't think either, I was just taking some photographs.'

He groaned some more, clutched at his shin and rolled back and forth a little.

At least he was able to move, and clearly he was able to breathe too.

'They never do think though, do they? The other road users and pedestrians who keep causing these types of accidents for us riders I mean.'

'Can I help you up?' I offered in my most sympathetic tone, my face squirming apologetically. He did not look amenable to my offer. 'Or let me get this bike out of your way then.'

I propped it up against the fence beside me and thanked the heavens there didn't appear to be any damage to it. I did not have the kind of money they'd likely look for to fix or even replace a thing like that.

To my great relief, he was able to get himself up, all be it slowly and with a bit of the dying swan act about him.

'I'm ok,' he said as he dusted himself off.

'I'm so relieved,' I said, while pretending I wasn't noticing the fine muscular form he made in those tight fighting sports clothes of his.

As he raised his eyes up to look at me before speaking again, I noticed how dreamy their deep chocolate brown colour was. Everything about him looked perfectly sun-kissed. Olive skin, and dark hair with some streaks of mid-brown flowing through it.

'What on earth were you thinking by just stepping down backwards on to the road like that?'

'I really wasn't thinking much at all, to be honest, and that's what's gone wrong there.'

'This is all people in the cycling community like me hear. You can't just ignore basic road rules, the cycling lane is still on a road. Would you just step out in front of a car?'

'Well, no,' I answered. 'But I suppose subconsciously I listen for those while near to the road, while you on the other hand, are all sort of super silent really.'

'That's why they teach you stop, and look as well as listen in primary school then. Isn't it?'

Good grief he's infantilising me ...

'I do not appreciate being spoken to as if I were either some type of imbecile or a child Mr,' then I paused unable to finish my sentence. I realised I was in the grip of outrage combined with PTSD from all of the other times in my life that members of the opposite sex had tried to devalue or belittle my existence in some way. I really didn't even know this particular latest male offender's name and it had all merged into years of hurt inside my head.

'Rutridge.'

'What?' I asked.

'That's my surname, Rutridge. Therefore, it's Mr Rutridge I believe you are trying to say next.'

'Yes, well,' I continued. 'Mr Rutridge, while I can see you are bleeding, inconvenienced and all, I am truly sorry I caused this accident, but I do not accept being spoken down to by anyone.'

He just stood there staring me straight in the face, blinking solidly.

'I really do feel awful though,' I went on. 'I checked your bike and that's alright. The bleeding on your leg worries me though; you might have some swelling come up on that leg too.'

'I'll be fine, best be getting on then,' he said.

'No, wait,' I blurted out as he moved towards his leaning bike. 'I have a house just there, you really must let me ensure those cuts are cleaned, and have you put some ice on that knee before you go. I don't want you getting an infection and needing to go on a course of antibiotics or something into the bargain.'

'Look, thank you for the offer and the concern, but I really must be getting on,' he moved to get back on his bike again.

'No, really, I must insist,' I surprised myself even with the strength of my conviction as I placed a hand on his arm to stop him mounting up on the cycle again. 'It would be wrong of me to let you walk away bleeding as you are still, just follow me please, come on.'

He relented, and nodded by way of a grudging 'alright' before following me back in to the house.

'So, I know your surname how, but how about your first name?' I said as we walked inside to my place, trying to clear the awkward air a little.

'It's Kane.'

'Pleased to meet you Kane,' I said. 'Just bring your bike right inside, I wouldn't want it to get stolen. Don't worry about the mess, the place is overdue another big clean.'

Straight-faced the whole time, he followed me inside, leaned his fancy bicycle just below one of the front windows, and took a seat on the couch.

'I'm not bleeding out any more at least,' he offered.

'Not to worry, I'll bring you out a clean cloth with some warm soapy water on it. I'm not sure I have anything like antiseptic cream or the like around, since there's no-one actually living in here at the moment, but the soap and water will be enough for now, and you might want to put some more of that cream on later when you get home, just to be on the safe side.'

'My, aren't you the good little nurse?' he said looking a bit impressed.

'I try,' I said. I could feel myself flirting a bit already and reminded myself to have some self-control, after all, I wasn't even through my self-pity party over what Ali did to me yet.

After he'd cleaned himself up, I offered him some water. He took some, it was always a welcome thing in the Queensland summer heat.

'Is this your place then?' he asked as he drank down the cool glass of water – I had found some ice left behind in the freezer to make it so. The taps in Queensland spit out tepid water at this time of year after all.

'I'm the joint owner, so yes, I suppose. But I don't live here or anything, no plans to either.'

'Oh, I see,' his expression and something in the tone almost seemed to turn to disapproval again.

'Do you live around here?'

'Yes, as a matter of fact, I do. I love this area. St. Lucia has been home to me since my days studying in the engineering school over there at UQ. Couldn't think of anywhere in this city I'd rather live.'

'It is a beautiful suburb,' I said agreeably. 'One of my parents spent their early years here, this was my Gran and Grandad's first family home.'

'You inherited it then?'

'That's right,' I confirmed. 'Me and my cousin are the joint owners now. Both of our grandparents who originally bought this place are no longer around. My Gran only just recently passed away this year, so I'm still feeling a bit sad and nostalgic about the whole thing, and our ownership of the place is hence fairly recent too.'

'It really makes you take stock a death in the family.'

'It really does.'

'So, the next thing I'm sure you will be getting on with is fixing up what needs urgent attention around here.'

'Um,' I hesitated to answer him because I was confused. 'The house is in excellent condition, we just aim to rent it out to Uni students, so it doesn't need to be super flashy or have top end fitments or the like. Everything's functional'.

'Well, I find that's typical of the sort of things landlords always say. In particular to people like me who live in the area themselves. I noticed on the way in that the stumps are starting to slump on one side of the house; it'll need re-stumping fairly soon. If you put it off, you might find issues with sticking doors and windows and the like. Then there is the fact that there appeared to be one or two tiles looking loose up on that roof. If a big storm comes in, that whole thing could be off; it could start a leak inside your roof, or worse still, injure someone down below. Then there's the gutters, they have holes in them. That's not storm smart. Oh, and the paint's starting to peel off in places on the weatherboards outside.'

I felt like putting a hand over his mouth and just hushing him as he ran through that list of all my little house's short-comings, as he so evidently saw it.

Suddenly I was feeling quite pleased he would be leaving imminently. Beautiful as he was to gaze upon, he had really put a dampener on my mood for the day.

'Well, I'm glad you seem to be fine now. Have a nice rest of your trip, and hopefully you don't bump into any more accident-prone people like me today.'

I think he sensed he had taken the negativity a step too far for me. Saying he was embarrassed as such would be an over-statement, but he did have the grace to avert his eyes downward, presumably realising what he said wasn't at all nice.

'Yes, I won't take up your time any longer, ah …', then he realised he hadn't actually gotten my name from me. 'What was your name then?'

'I'm Meg.'

'Thank you, Meg, I seem to be good to go.'

'Take care then,' and I saw him out of the door.

It had felt nice to have some company for a brief while. I realised though that I suppose I was taking a bit of a chance inviting a strange man I didn't know into a house where I was totally alone, but I didn't sense anything at all dangerous about him. There was no reason to question the genuineness of the situation I met him in either. I certainly had just stepped right in front of him, that was a real tumble he took from that bike.

12:55pm By this hour, I realised I had done all the checking of the inside of the house that I could do. And as for the outside, well, not having any trades related skills whatsoever, there wasn't likely much for me to see, beyond the obvious.

Some of Kane's comments did still weigh on my mind. I promptly filed that all into the too hard for now category though, and went back to planning instead how I could do some little interior projects to spruce things up a bit. That way, we might even be able to raise the rent a little.

The main goal for me was to go back to my, once again single, professional girl's life in Sydney, feeling I had accomplished something during my stay up here in Brisbane.

Chapter Five

The 15th of December

9:30am Tucking in to some eggs Benedict at Merlos on the lovely UQ campus, I noticed how the perfume from the trees everywhere actually scented the air. It was all rather whimsical.

I hadn't come around here much in my own student days. That was since I was a QUT student, and hence always so busy out there in the city that I never thought of taking the time to check this place out. There was plenty to do around the city campus, even if there was not quite so much actually inside the campus. I can see how ideal it would be for the likes of an arts student of some kind, the historic setting being so conducive to concentration, imagination and delving into contemplations about the past or other worlds. But for someone like me who studied a more practical course of marketing, a city campus, like the one QUT sits on, was actually very appropriate. I would see real city worker types suited up and making their way to their offices in the morning rush, and out on lunch breaks. It always reminded me that's what I was working towards in my own studies. Made me more grounded I think, and already in the right type of mindset and routine by the time I actually hit the office space as a graduate.

I was, for the first time in my life however, questioning just how sensible my sensible approach to life really was in the grand scheme of things. I mean, I was sitting here in my 30s, only having some property to my name because my grandparents left me some, and currently with no relationship or children even anywhere on the horizon.

Then a happy sight for sore eyes snapped me out of my melancholy somewhat. I tried to make out his name from his lapel badge, but I was too shortsighted. He was the perfect Italian café staff member. Beautiful tanned skin and chiselled features with dark hair that make him look like he'd just stepped out of one of those movies in the Italian film festivals they have at the cinema every year.

He started looking at me, I think he realised I was staring. I gave him a rather flirtatious and cheeky smile, couldn't help myself.

He started flirting back, 'I'll be right over to get those plates out of your way,' he said when he really didn't have to. A bit mischievous and even more handsome looking as he did so.

I just smiled back coyly. When he came over to clear my table, he brushed my arm gently with his, deliberately, I liked to think.

But no sooner had I started drifting up in my mind towards cloud nine, when I suddenly found myself crashing rapidly.

He looked as surprised as I was when a young glamourous, skinny and leggy twenty something with the blondest of blonde hair turned up, to start a shift too presumably, and walked over and kissed him. I saw her eyeing me off a little, well, as far as I could see with my short-sightedness that was. She was definitely looking over towards me. She would likely have seen him getting rather close to me and hovering around a bit while carrying out his table clearing duties. That was what he was up to as she was walking around towards us through the beautiful majestic old sandstone cloisters. It was like I had never existed then, never another glance anywhere near my direction from him after that.

Were men truly all just the very same?

10:30am Arrived back to the garden gate of our little house. It was a fairly short and pleasant walk to our little rental property from UQ. Had one last look around the house and decided that the only DIY project I could realistically do within the few weeks of sick leave I had was to paint all of the internal walls. Freshen things up a bit.

One feature of the post-war homes that made that very feasible, even for me, was the fact that the ceilings weren't too high in these houses. Not like the old traditional Queenslander styles. I could reach all the corners in here, and the walls were simple and flat, making them so super easy to paint. Besides, I had read once that sprucing up the paint around a house is the cheapest and easiest DIY upgrade a landlord can do for the highest expected return in rental yield. I guess it figures that it's much more inviting when you walk into a place and it all looks neat, crisp and clean.

12:35pm Found Indooroopilly Bunnings, the inner-city hardware mecca. The paint shop was impressively extensive even though it was a smaller urban store. After about an hour of browsing, I left with several tester pots of various trendy shades, though they were mostly variants of white and cream, had some modern greys in there too.

That should keep me busy for a while.

3:00pm It does start to get a bit cooler at this time of day at least. Had gone all around the house holding up paint colour cards and trying to plan what I would put where. Now was time to put tired feet up with a cuppa out on the humble little outdoor setting in the back yard.

Again, at this point I began appreciating the wonder of the Queensland family home with fresh eyes. We were so far away from our neighbours with a big grassy block laid out around me. Had forgotten what this level of own un-invaded personal space felt like after so many years living down in Sydney. It almost seemed just a little lonely at times though, I guess just because I was no longer used to it.

3:20pm Blissful peace of the backyard with the predominant sound being the birds chirping, was interrupted with a buzz from my mobile.

THIS IS A CURTESY TEXT TO INFORM YOU THAT YOUR RECENT TESTS DONE AT OUR CLINIC HAVE ALL CAME BACK NEGATIVE.

Thank God.

I breathed a huge sigh of relief. At least Ali hadn't left me with any nasty medical surprises into the bargain. When this broken heart of mine has mended, I can face the world again with no other lingering ongoing issues.

4:00pm Realised I had become so relaxed and comfortable, forgetting the world and all that, that I had just sat here and daydreamed for ages. The online ordering of the paint was something I could do this evening when back at cousin Tilly's place, so I decided just to allow myself to enjoy this moment.

The strangest thoughts started drifting into my mind then. Perhaps it was because I stopped to read a few plaques and other things on the wall while over at UQ for my breakfast and it had stirred my imagination, but I, for some reason, started pondering about the founders of that place, and how they came to choose this particular little nook down river from the main site of the burgeoning colonial era city to become the campus.

UQ was right in the centre of the city originally, close to where the state parliament sits these days. City life just over a century ago when they began founding it wasn't all it was cracked up to be though. It certainly was not so fun as it is nowadays. I recall reading once that offensive odours were one of the biggest problems in Brisbane's earlier years. That, coupled with there not being any air conditioning, rather drives home how in fact torturous much of the place would have been to work in during the summer in particular. And even in most of the spring and autumn as well.

Indeed, this little hamlet sat on the pocket of land enveloped most of the way around by the snaking river, would really have been quite the little paradise to escape from it all. Much like how I was feeling by being here at the moment, putting the excesses of Sydney and excesses of life among the city's high fliers and biggest scoundrels behind me.

4:20pm Heard the sound of a door being opened, and looked to the next-door yard to see Matt coming out into their back patio.

'Hi Matt,' I yelled over.

'How are you going?' he replied.

'Not too badly,' I said. 'I have spent today planning a new paint colour scheme for the interior of the house. That's the little project I've decided on to keep me occupied for the duration of my stay up here.'

'Good idea,' said Matt, kindly. 'That's quite manageable, and it always encourages renters to consider a place if the paint is fresh and in a modern colour scheme. No-one wants to feel like they've moved in with their grandparents or something.'

I felt myself chuckle slightly at that.

'Will it be a busy time for you over the December period then?'

'Well, because I'm here with funding support from a rural students' scheme, I have some interesting placement options I can do over the summer. One of them is in a physio practise out in Charleville which isn't too far from the farm I grew up on. I'm flying out there in two days' time in fact because I'll be doing some shadowing work in the lead up to Christmas for a 5-day practical immersion. From there I'll head out to my parents' place for the whole family gathering. There should be about 30 or so of us all together for Christmas lunch.'

'Sounds lovely,' I said having one of those wistful moments of imagining myself having a big old fashioned country family around me. Still, cousin Tilly, one and only cousin, as she is to me, is pretty good company all by herself.

'I'm still quite surprised no-one has snapped your place up by now given the location. We got some worrying news the other day; the owners of this place are looking to sell now. Don't know what that'll mean for us, it'll be in the New Year most likely. I'm surprised because it's an easy convenient little investment for them. We pay good rent, always on time and with no trouble.'

'Maybe it's just personal circumstances.'

'Who knows for sure, but I just find it all a bit odd for reasons I can't quite put my finger on. Something I had noticed though, in the last 6 months in particular, is that they seem to be having more trouble getting repairs done and that sort of thing. It's meant to be the real estate manager who deals with it all, and it never seemed to be a problem in the past.'

'Maybe it's just because of this building boom that's been going on, making it hard in general to find tradies who are not otherwise engaged at eye-watering rates on some big scale project.'

'Maybe,' said Matt scrunching his face up a little. 'Or maybe it's some type of dodgy Brisbane real-estate agent trick or scam going down.'

Hadn't heard stories like that for while now, but as he brought the issue up, memories did come flooding back to me hearing complaints over the years past about the untrustworthiness, and in fact oftentimes outright criminality of the estate agent world here.

'Maybe they've got a developer or something lined up to scoop up our place and even some others nearby, so it suits them to make it less convenient for the current owners here to hold on to this little spot and keep renting it out like this. Come to think on it, it could explain why your place is conspicuously sitting empty as well, there's meant to be a housing shortage after all, isn't there?'

I felt a creepy shiver across my neck when he made that connection between our two situations. Sadly, it was just all too possible as an explanation.

'The estate agents are meant to be coming around here within the next week and a half. The other house mates have already left the city until after Christmas, and in two days I won't be around either. That means they'll have the run of the place to come in and look around and do whatever they do in these situations. So, like making bids for representing it and the like I suppose,' continued Matt.

'Well, I guess I'll see them around then whilst I'm over here painting.'

'Most likely. If I don't see you before I take off, have a good Christmas.'

'Oh, thank you Matt, I will do. It's been really lovely being back home for Christmas.'

Chapter Six

The 16th of December

7:05am Admiring the lovely view from the train window as it smoothly glided out of the city, having just passed through the Southern suburbs and now down towards the Gold Coast.

Felt good knowing that since I had put through my paint order with Bunnings online last night, I could expect it all to be delivered to the door tomorrow. From then on it would be full days of hard work dedicated to painting until it was all completed. Today would be all about me relaxing.

9:15am Made sure to smother myself in sunscreen, because even though it was before 10am, the Queensland sun was already high in the sky and feeling pretty strong.

Hardest thing now was going to be resisting the urge to run straight into the water. Must wait that full 20 minutes to be sure the sunscreen is fully absorbed and working to protect me from skin cancer. So, 10 more minutes to go and counting …

9:45am Had been happily bobbing around peacefully for ages, when suddenly the swell started to get bigger and stronger. I felt reassured since I was swimming between the flags and could make out the bright yellow and red uniforms on the life savers in the tower on the beach, but the tide had begun to shift. It was now always sweeping me off to one side requiring a fair bit of effort to get back to where I started from and wanted to be.

The waves were turning a little bit dumpy as well. Hadn't seen that written on their chalk board with the conditions to expect for the day.

Increasingly, I started to find that when they came over my head, they were pushing me downwards, dumping down on me as it were. Then when I resurfaced, I would notice I'd been drastically shifted over to the left from where I had been.

Caught sight of monster wave significantly larger than the rest heading my way. Realised I couldn't outswim it so I began preparing to dive under or through it, as we all get advised.

Sadly, it didn't quite work out for me, however.

I felt the wave lift me up at first, then come up over my head, after which I felt like I was trapped in some larger than life washing machine. I really was not sure any more about which way was up.

Then, I felt my legs getting tangled in between other human legs. Again, they came from all directions it seemed, so they could be mistaken for tentacles or something. I could even feel that they were hairy.

When I finally got back upright, feet firmly wedged in the sinking sand of the ocean bed below me, I saw a bronzed smooth broad chest of a man right before my eyes. *Must be the owner of those over reaching hairy legs. Not very sun smart is he, out here without a rashie on, and in the height of summer too.*

I lifted my gaze, and to my amazement, it was none other than Kane, the man I sent flying off his bike the other day, standing right before me.

He looked rather cross with me, once again. He was rubbing his jaw.

'Well, that surely hurt,' he said immediately.

'What hurts?' I said back feeling a gentle sway as the now considerably smaller waves brushed into me, and then softly broke around me as they crawled up onto the beach.

'This part of my jaw you just kicked me in.'

'Oh,' I said rather sheepishly. 'I wasn't even aware of making contact with anyone's jaw.'

'Well, Meg,' he said in a tone more befitting a school teacher dealing with a naughty child. 'That's why people are taught to dive under waves, and just in general, to have some care to take in who is around you when out enjoying the surf.'

'It's not at all easy to be aware of what is around you when you get picked up then dumped on by a powerful ocean wave,' I said sounding somewhat like a petulant school child. *He was doing it again, infantilising me.*

'Yes, and that's precisely why one is supposed to anticipate the waves while bathing within the busy areas between the flags, then dive into the wave if a large one is coming up.'

'Then please accept my sincerest apologies,' I said trying not to sound too sarcastic. 'I can assure you that my wrapping my legs around you, was in no way deliberate.'

I was quite sure I saw an almost seedy type of half smile creep across his face at that point.

Then I saw something resembling Pamela Anderson, as she used to look back in the 80s, coming towards us. The main difference was that the woman approaching us had a Gold Coast glitter strip style bikini on rather than that now classic all red one-piece from Baywatch. Her breasts were so over sized and plump in comparison to the rest of her body, that it was hard to see how that strappy, flimsy little bikini top held them both up there as they did. But it was certainly managing it somehow.

After a few swift strides from the spot where she had been standing on the shore, she dipped gracefully into the small lapping waves at the line where the sand bank dropped off underfoot, and swiftly swam over to us like an Olympian.

'Kane, are you alright?' she said reaching for his jaw and stroking it lovingly. 'I saw that you were rubbing the side of your face and thought, poor Kane! That wave was such a big one.'

Just swallow me up whole now please ocean. I am ready to go.

'I dare say I'll survive,' he said to her while throwing a side glance towards me.

'Oh, this is Meg, Carolyn,' he said to her. 'She's rather accident prone; we met just the other day when she caused me to fall off of my bike by stepping out right in front of me as I was cycling past her house.'

She seriously looked at me as if I had two heads, then wrapped both her arms around Kane while making some pouting face as if she had to help shield him from me.

How pathetic.

Having been away from life in Queensland for quite some time, I had forgotten the way some younger women and girls around here get so possessive of 'their men' that they act like any other woman being spoken to by them is a threat of some kind. I remember putting it down to the massive popularity of single-sex educational establishments in the past. Wonder if that is the reason though, or if it's just something peculiar about the dating culture in the sunshine state.

'Nice to bump into you again, I'm sure,' said Kane.

'Yes, likewise,' was all I could manage. I next attempted to swim stylishly towards the beach again in a reverse version of what Kane's lady friend had just done. Then, as it didn't feel just so smooth as I had intended, I decided to just stand up, awkward as it was, and do a far less graceful wade back.

When I got to the shore, I gave a glance back in Kane's direction, and to my surprise, he appeared to be looking back at me. *Did he watch me all the way?* His girlfriend was still wrapped tightly all around him.

I was relieved to find no-one had pinched any of my stuff that I had just left lying on the beach. That's what us Queenslanders always did since we were kids, just leave everything unattended and trust it would all be fine. Having read about how Queensland was changing rapidly in recent times though, I wondered if that were still such a sensible thing to do.

11:30am It was rather early for lunch, but swimming does use up a lot of energy. Given I hadn't driven here, I was enjoying a nice crisp glass of Chardonnay while I waited for them to serve up my grilled barramundi and chips order – the taste of Queensland summer for me.

All sorts of lovely memories were dancing through my head. I thought of being here with the oldies so long ago. It was just so much fun that me and Tilly used to have down in this place.

Realised I was still too upset and raw to enjoy the romance novels that I usually love. I had brought with me a copy of something that promised to be an action-packed thriller to read by the coast. Maybe reading about people killing one another would distract me enough from my own pity party that I could finally just move on, or so I hoped.

12:15pm Decided to have caffeine after downing a couple of glasses of white. I ordered myself a double-shot cappuccino while I remained engrossed in my book. I had become quite settled in this spot in fact; it was perfectly placed along Surfer's beachfront strip so that I could feel the ocean breeze and even see its vast expanse on the horizon before me.

Popping my nose above my book for a moment though, I saw *him* again. It was Kane and that model-like creature strolling past hand in hand. He didn't notice me, and I felt thankful for that. Not quite sure why, but I just didn't want him to know I was yet again totally alone here. I was here with no-one for company, let alone a modelling-role-worthy other half, like he was running around with. *But why was I even caring though?*

3:35pm Back in Tilly's lovely central apartment, I was sitting with my feet curled up on the sofa beside me whilst flicking through Netflix.

Checked that everything was on track to be delivered to the house tomorrow and I would be a DIY powerhouse probably right up until Christmas itself.

6:10pm Cousin Tilly arrived home and began sharing her most fascinating tales about her arty friends during that day.

It really was a different world from what I was used to as a long-term office worker.

She was telling me of how one of the stage lighting crew was looking for a new place after a breakup with his girlfriend. They had owned and cared together for a set of guinea pigs that comprised two born of the same litter. They had already agreed that as part of the split, they each would take their own half of the little pair to their new respective places. So far so good one would think, but they were still haggling over ongoing arrangements for 'visitation' and 'access' to one another for the two little creatures. *I wish my problems in life were only as complex as that.*

8:00pm I decided to watch a Leonardo DiCaprio movie again – *The Great Gatsby* it was this time. I loved the fact that much of it was filmed in Sydney. I had even once joined the onlookers near the set to see if I could catch a glimpse of Leo himself when they were doing the filming there. My younger self never did see Leo in the flesh sadly, but I did meet a lovely English chap however. So at least I wasn't standing there all alone in the crowd for too long.

The ending of that movie still makes me cry so ... and today was no different.

To make it less painful, I try to take a less literal interpretation of the ending, when I can. Sometimes true love is about the biggest sacrifices, and when you think about it, even love between two people is always bigger than just them. Lying there in what looks more like a beautiful sleep than a final cold ending, I see how much the child is the father of the man, and vice-versa. And the green light ... well, that part reminds me rather of train lines. There's always a red light on when a train is coming into the station and is scheduled to make a stop – while if it's green, then the train carries on, past the station, and out of reach of anything or anyone which might have been waiting there to end such unspoiled and noble dreams.

Chapter Seven

The 17th of December

7:22am Heard the sound of a truck outside. The paint and brushes etc delivery was right on time.

Decided to head out to meet them as they were unloading. Always best to check for any errors in the order before they just whizz off.

The truck was straddling the verge of the nature strip and the road. Two blokes had already begun bringing things out from the back and lopping them onto the pavement by the gate.

"Morning," I said to them cheerfully as I headed out.

"G'day," one of them replied. The other nodded at me.

I hope you don't mind, but do you have a detailed inventory there that I can just check against what you've brought?

The thinner of the two men paused and looked up sidewards for a moment, then said, 'Sure thing.'

All in an instant, he spritely spun on one heel and round the front side of the van towards the driver's side door.

Then I heard the yell.

Not again.

The other man let out a groan followed by 'You right there mate?'.

I rushed towards the front end of the van too, in order to see what had happened. And there he was, once again – it was Kane.

The thin delivery man was already busy helping him up while also clearing him and his bike out of the way of the oncoming cars. Some had slowed and come to a stop to avoid hitting him.

'I just nipped round so fast like to grab something from the door pouch. The lady here had asked to see our itemised delivery ledger,' I could hear him explaining to Kane.

At that moment, Kane, looking up from a bent over position with hands on his knees while catching his breath and trying to regain some calmness, glared at me furiously. The intent stare seemed as if to say *I can't believe you've done this to me for a second time.*

Don't blame me! My head was screaming. This really was not my fault, but it was darned bad luck. They say lightning never strikes twice, not in this place though.

'Oh Kane,' I blurted out. 'Are you alright, I'm so sorry this seems to have happened to you once again.'

The delivery man shot me a confused look.

'This is Kane,' I said to him, feeling I had to explain myself and introduce him as if we were out having cocktails and canapes together. 'We met recently when he had a fall from his bike at this exact same spot.'

Suddenly the workmen both seemed to be ready to transfer responsibility for the latest accident on to poor Kane himself. I felt a little bad about that, but it is a common plight suffered by the cycling community as I understand it.

'Aw mate, you gotta be careful when you're on the roads, take care to avoid hazards and that,' the suddenly less apologetic one who had been standing beside him said to Kane.

'Just didn't see ya mate, all so fast,' the other who was responsible added, in a tone that now signalled a subtle agreement with an unspoken ruling that Kane was at fault for what had happened to him.

Again, his bike seemed to be ok, which was a relief. He didn't appear bloodied this time, but he was clutching at his head, then shaking it as if slightly dazed which I was a little bit worried about.

'Can I bring you inside again?' I said.

Kane quickly nodded a reluctant yes.

My, he must really be feeling bad.

7:45am The workmen had quickly cleared off, and in the end, after all the commotion, I hadn't even checked the order. I noticed they'd placed the invoice listing all of the items under one of the paint tubs which they stacked into a pile inside the little hallway entrance of this old house. I just hoped everything had arrived. There would be more time to worry about it later on if it hadn't.

Right now, I was somewhat in a daze looking upon Kane lying stretched out on the living room lounge. He was a bit overly sweaty for my tastes currently, and badly in need of a shower, but I was still finding myself drawn to noticing his fine chiselled abs outlined by the tight Lycra. As for the rest, well, I tried not to look that far down for decency's sake, though it was tempting.

Letting his eyelids become heavy, I noticed he was starting to look like he might drift off to sleep. Remembering about the only thing I could recall from workplace health and safety training over the years, I knew in case of possible concussion after any knock to the head, it's important not to let the patient go to sleep.

'I hope you're not nodding off there,' I said as I placed the glass of water I had just fetched for him down on the side table.

'I do feel a little light headed, that's all. It has probably just been the fright I got again.'

'Hopefully that's all,' I said. 'But you do have to be careful anytime when you might have hit your head. I'd prefer if you stay alert just in case.'

'I'm trying,' he said while sitting up and taking the glass of water into his hands.

'You know what,' I said suddenly, 'you really should go up and take a shower. That'll freshen you up and wake you up a bit, I think. You'll feel better prepared to set off again as well.'

'I don't really want to be that much of an imposition,' he said sighing.

'It's no problem at all, really,' I reassured him. 'The house is a rental, and it's untenanted currently, so it's not like you'd be disturbing anyone at all.'

He mulled it over for a moment whilst taking some more of the water then said, 'You know what, I think I'll take you up on that offer.'

'I'll go fetch you a towel then', I said. I brought one over with me, you can borrow it for now.'

As I returned with the towel from my bag, I could see Kane looking around the room.

'This will all be painted a modern cool grey.'

'Sounds lovely,' Kane said approvingly.

'So, still no luck finding tenants then?' he asked me.

'Nope.'

'You know, I have seen estate agents out and about around this suburb with developers in tow in the last few months.'

'But it seems so developed around here already, surely the council wouldn't be approving any more.'

'They can always find a way to cram in more and more though when they see there's decent profits to be made. Look at the scary over developed mess they made out of the once quite lovely family suburb of Indooroopilly. It has at least three waves of peak traffic periods per day now. It's reached the point they've built what looks like a motorway fly over just to get around the shopping centre.'

That did make me laugh a little, but really, it was not at all funny. A small group of people we had trusted to manage our suburbs truly had made it far less liveable and pleasant than it used to be even just a short decade ago.

I started to realise then, that maybe there was something rather suspicious behind our agent's claims to be unable to find a tenant for us still.

8:15am Could hear that Kane seemed to be out of the shower. I was so relieved he was ok for the second time around ... did get me thinking on whether fate was for some reason bringing us to meet each other over and over. But if so, then why?

8:30am He finally came back into the lounge looking fresh once more, and smelling clean.

'Well, I'd better be on my way then. I told my work I would just work from home today, but best be getting back to mine then before much more of the morning rolls on.'

'Oh, of course,' I said rising to my feet and moving towards the door to show him out.

That was when it happened though, and all so quickly.

I could see and feel him from the side moving awkwardly such that he was coming more towards me than alongside me to leave. I felt soft wet lips brushing against my own, just tentatively at first, then before I could even stop to think, we were locked in a passionate lengthy kiss.

Then, as soon as it was over, and he was looking at me softly, I just ruined it all with: 'Oh, but you have a girlfriend, don't you?'

Why did I say that at that moment? So stupid and worthy of a high-schooler.

His face fell like a stone sinking to the bottom of a river.

'Well, I do apologise then,' he said awkwardly with his face reddening and just promptly walked straight out of the door saying nothing more.

Damn it.

1pm I had hoped that by now I would be feeling calmer about what had happened in the morning with Kane, but I wasn't.

I was still reliving the moment over and over in my mind, and thinking of how I could have said something far smarter and appropriate to the situation.

And his girlfriend, I mean, she was so stuck up that she didn't even acknowledge me that day on the beach.

It's not that I support cheating, or dream of getting with a cheater, but really, there was no reason for me even to just assume that Kane was still with that woman. They could have broken up since I saw him last, and now, I might never know.

What if I never ever see him again?

Chapter Eight

The 18th of December

10:23am Had made a good start this morning and it was amazing how much of the living room was covered in a clean, bright, white prep coat already.

The secret of true happiness in this life is learning how to appreciate the little things, I think.

Finding painting is so much easier now than can recall from childhood. No more need for foul smelling oil-based paints that spin your head if you breathe them in too much and need turpentine if you spill them on anything by mistake. Loving the ease of being able to just put my brushes into plain old water to get them clean again.

On the down side, whenever I did pause for a break, Kane kept popping into my head. I was wondering what he was up to right now. Was he back with that slim and trim glamourous girlfriend? It had felt so good when he held me close like that, just for that fleeting moment.

Must put distracting thoughts out of head.

The 19th of December

11:45am Realised I was getting peckish already. Not used to so much physical exercise of a morning, and it was the second day in a row that I would be spending alternating between being on my feet and crouching down in the squat position for literally hours.

Really hope I have harder hotter buns after this. Would be nice if I could have two lasting achievements when I go back down to Sydney after this sick leave.

Forgot to pack some food to bring with me today for lunch, so Merlos over at UQ campus was looking like a good option again.

Mustn't spoil myself too much, but lunch there surrounded by so much cool and imposing stone, as well as those old and reliable trees, was just so relaxing. I deserved it.

Besides, it would be nice to have some human interaction for a short while. Other than that, I could find I just end up talking to these walls I've been painting all day until I see cousin Tilly when she gets home after her work this evening.

1pm This Merlos café food really did bring to mind my travels in Italy. I was thinking of the time I spent a week in Florence, and then did some odd jobs in various Tuscan countryside spots. Those were the days.

I tried to remind myself that not that much had changed since then really. Magic is always around you in life, you just have to seek it out. True it was, that having aged slightly since then, I was past the stage where a flick of the hair or flirty glance from me while I carelessly slid a hand along my lithe 20 something body would be met with almost guaranteed reciprocation. But there was so much more to life than all that, after all.

One thing I have found as the years ticked by, is that whilst I started to feel increasingly less like mere eye candy for passing admirers with each year that came and went, at the same time, I was getting more mature and caring less.

1:15pm Sipping on my coffee now, I found that Kane kept jumping back into my mind, much as I tried to push all thoughts of him out. What good would it do after all? I had screwed up the chance of finding out if there might have been something there. I was quite certain I had done so at least. Why did I say that? What a stupid comment: Oh, well. We can't go back in time.

After the recurrent disappointment feeling passed, next came thoughts that were more, well, paranoid frankly. My mind was running off on tangents. Sure, Kane seemed at face value to be so highly principled, and caring about the good of our suburb, disapproving of developers' greed and all that, but what if he's in fact a scammer, and involved with the developers? It was strange how we kept bumping into each other after all. Three times no less.

I couldn't help myself from entertaining such thoughts for a few moments, but then I returned to a more reasonable mental space. He really did look like he had two genuine tumbles from his bike. Besides, I don't even fully own a property, I'm just a half owner, so there's no sure guarantee of anything that worthwhile as a pay off at the end for a scammer who might target me.

That thought comforted me somewhat.

I had felt guilty even thinking these things, but then I reminded myself that I was being sensible really by not just accepting things at face value no matter how polite or respectable someone you meet seems. You really can't tell. Look at what just happened to me with Ali. I really felt I had gotten close to him and knew him well.

Many people were never that trustworthy all throughout the history of humankind though. I hold the belief that the world goes in and out of phases where that type of problem is more heightened than at other times. Right now felt like we were all in the middle of a rough patch in a social sense. There had been such rapid societal change for us all to face within a relatively short time period. *Australia was growing up* was what they'd tell us a couple of decades ago. The population was to move to *large,* as if those of us here just weren't quite good enough as we were, for whatever reason. Then that was followed by massive boom times leading people to suddenly become obsessed with future financial planning even if they'd never thought much of it before. Then next came Covid, and a weakening of the economy leaving most ordinary folks struggling to make their mortgage repayments and having to weigh up the need for fruit and veg in a weekly shop as the prices meant it was becoming a luxury.

I suppose this climate was ripe times for the scammers looking at us *have gots*, as they must see us, and thinking about how they could go about transferring what we have away from us over to themselves. For that reason, I figured I was sensible to always keep some degree of caution in all interactions.

Still, on the balance of probabilities, it seemed like Kane was probably not a scammer who was only trying to find a way to get to talk to me. Then going so far as even passionately kissing me, all just to get at Gran and Grandad's old home, their life savings basically.

The 20ᵗʰ of December

10:55am Another room in this old house was now well under way towards being fully refreshed and brought up to modern times in terms of colour scheme. Amazing what some new paint can do. I feel better already when walking through the main living areas after my hard work so far.

11:25am Went out to sit in the back yard to take a coffee when I heard a rather strange sound coming from next door. Somewhat of a high-pitched squeal was how I would describe it.

I thought about ignoring it. Then my curiosity got the better of me, so I decided to poke my nose over the little wooden fence whereupon I was confronted with the strangest thing – skimpy, lacy, sexy, black lingerie discarded on the grass.

What on earth now?

This really could not be described as usual for any place, and for a brief moment I feared someone had been sexually assaulted in the neighbours' yard. Matt must have been long gone back to the country for his UQ regional placement combined with his private Christmas visit to family by now.

What if someone is in there all tied up and in need of help, or worse, there's a dead body inside?

11:27am The minutes were moving by fast, because they felt so critical since the scary thoughts of dead or injured persons potentially being right next door to me whilst I was here all alone had come into my mind.

I had made a resolve to act however. I was going to have to go over there and check it out.

Made my way back inside my place, then went out the front gate and over in through the next-door neighbours' gate. I could see there was some mail piling up in their letter box outside already, but from the yard, everything appeared to be locked up and in good order. The front windows were too high up for me to try to peer inside.

There was nothing blocking me from moving around to the back of the yard so I went around to take a look.

I was soon confronted with yet more discarded underwear - it was gent's undies this time. A pair of briefs just lying on the back decking at the foot of the stairs up to the back side of the house where I could see a door had been left open. They weren't just your regular bonds cottons men's briefs or something though, they really seemed to be something quite special – Italian silk boxers fit for any Italian stallion, or wannabe.

Had my next-door neighbours' home turned into a pop-up brothel overnight since they'd all left town for the holidays or something?

I knew I was going to have to pluck up the courage to go up there and see if anyone was in trouble because this was plain weird and frankly very concerning.

I had become very conscious of the fact that I was totally alone though. My sense of self-preservation having become heightened when the signs left in the trail of discarded personal items suggested there could still be a dangerous male stranger inside there.

11:35am After pacing around a little bit and using my ears to see if I could pick up any sounds coming from inside, though that was largely too interrupted by my picking up all the traffic noise drifting around from the busy road out front to be of much use, I decided to deftly and quietly creep up the stairs to get closer.

There was no sign of anyone in there, and it didn't seem wise to call out. I wanted to know who, or what, was potentially inside before alerting them to my own presence.

I took the plunge and stepped inside, then as I drew closer to the hallway, I thought I heard something that sounded like a thud on the floor above. This house was a two-story brick that looked like it was built in the 70s or thereabouts, so there was farther to explore still, and I made my way up the functional carpeted stairs. The carpet underfoot disguised the sound of my climbing them.

Then I saw them both from a concealed spot partially shielded by the top landing wall, the two that were inside. They were both completely naked and having sex on the bathroom floor. Thankfully their faces were turned away from me. The woman was young and perfect looking. Her golden hued skin and petite frame matched her Asian appearance, and she lay partially on her side with the broad young muscular male on top of her.

It was then that the flashbacks started – this was just too disturbingly similar to the scene I walked in on when Ali was sleeping with those two professional women behind my back – and I began getting a pulsing, squeezing headache and seeing flashes of light before my eyes. My head had started to quickly turn dizzy too and I feared I might just fall over and tumble back down the stairs.

What is it with people having bathroom sex at times when they're meant to be doing other regular mundane things these days?

This was all just too much and far too overwhelming for me right now. I was still in recovery mode from Ali, and this was the very last thing I had needed to see.

I knew the two I saw were both safe and consenting to what was happening in here this morning – that much was clear with the sounds coming from them getting loud now - so I was happy to head back out as quickly, but quietly, as possible. I had done my duty of checking no-one that needed any help.

When I got back down into the lower level of the house, I noticed what I guessed must have been more of the belongings of those two going at it like wild rabbits long deprived of company upstairs there. I felt a little guilty because I decided to slightly open the briefcase that had been discarded to see if there was any clue as to whom it belonged.

When I saw who it belonged to, that guilt was gone. For just like a secret agent during wartime reconnaissance or the like, this was something that I had to find out about, and had every right to know about – they were estate agents. Saturdays are meant to be their peak property inspection days for prospective tenants. No doubt they were the very ones meant to be looking after this property right now, and ensuring a seamless transition to a new owner for the landlord, which would also ensure no disruption to Matt and our other lovely neighbours.

I fully admit it had all felt like some big conspiracy when I first heard people talking about the inherent evil in developers and those who partner with them in local business, but I could see now that these people were the enemy. There really was no nicer way to put it.

5:48pm Tilly came home through the door. I was bursting to tell her what I had caught the estate agents next door doing.

'You actually caught them in there, just having a sex romp together, presumably on the neighbour's time and dime while they were meant to be finding buyers for that place?' she said to me once I told her what had happened that day while I was over working at the rental house.

'Basically. Yes.'

Her face was revealing to me that she was just utterly stunned.

'They are so unscrupulous,' she went on. 'And I am starting to believe too now that there could be some bigger conspiracy going on with them colluding together to help force people out to get deals for big developers paying them backhanders.'

'It would not be the first time sadly,' I agreed, sighing heavily.

'But what are we going to do about it then?'

'I don't know really at this stage, I mean, they're not our estate agents after all, and we have no proof we've been getting cheated. Although it is strange that we don't have any new tenant interest given our situation.'

'I know there's no proof of any wrongdoing yet,' conceded Tilly, 'But it would seem a little unwise to just ignore this. Maybe we should set a deadline. Like if they don't have a new tenant, or someone in the pipeline at least by mid-January next year, we reconsider our options?'

'I think that would be sensible.'

The 21st of December

8:30am Proud of ourselves this morning, Tilly and I were already half way climbed up the Mount Coot-tha walking trail by this early time of day. Much as I was enjoying the tranquil surroundings, particularly the way the breeze could be heard dancing through the thin spindly trees all around and the sound of traffic was entirely absent. I was looking forward to some eggs Bennie at the café at the lookout atop the hill.

The sense of history of this place had never been lost on me either. This, back in the early days of the city of Brisbane as we know it today, was always the in place to have picnics, even wedding celebrations and other important gatherings. It sent shivers down my spine when I imagined how a group of Victorian settlers, probably many still sporting their native Scottish or English accents, might have stood on the very same spots around slaughter falls, or up at the peak of the hill, perhaps gathered around a little baby born in 18 hundred and something or other, and not surprisingly we still do similar things to this very day.

8:45am Reached the top. Don't know why, but even after I have seen it so many times, the way the view of the city comes into sight when one rounds the little mound at the top after the quiet walk through the trees still always takes my breath away.

9:10am By now we were both heartily tucking into our Sunday breakfast treat. The heat was on the rise of course, and the humidity too, as another hot summer's day had just been born over our city. The walk down wasn't too hard however, and it was always pretty cool on that track because it was so mercifully naturally shaded.

'I just realised that you haven't gotten around to going to the beach yet since I got here,' I announced quite suddenly.

'Oh yeah,' said Tilly. 'But, you know, I hardly go at all these days. Pretty sad, isn't it?'

'Indeed. Well, why don't we just go this arvo?'

Tilly looked at me as if I had suggested something strange.

'It's only an easy train and tram ride away to the Goldie now,' I said encouragingly.

'True, but we've had such a big morning,' whined Tilly. 'We're not the spring chickies we used to be any more!'

'Speak for yourself,' I retorted playfully.

'How about this instead,' she suggested as a compromise. 'Why don't we agree that we will make the trek out to spend Christmas day on the beach, so a real old-fashioned Queensland style Christmas.'

'I would love that,' I said, 'We can have a traditional BBQ, take a pop-up beach shade, make a real day of it. It'll be just like old times.'

'Agreed, it's a deal then. And as for today, while I don't have the energy to do the full beach and bathing thing, I would be interested in hoping on the train out to the Bayside. We could go to Manly or somewhere. We could take an evening stroll and then go for a nice seafood dinner along the shoreline. Sound good?'

'Perfect. Sunday is sorted then, and tomorrow, I'll be back to work to make sure I get all that painting finished before it's time to head back down to Sydney.'

Chapter Nine

The 22nd of December

9:30am Back to the reno project this morning. I was well underway with my current task of using my exciting new tile paint product which the local Bunning's staff had so helpfully introduced me to. I couldn't believe it; it was like new tiles that you can just paint on! Covered up all of the discoloured grout spots too.

But then, my beautiful moment where I was proudly admiring my work so far, was rudely interrupted by a knock at the door.

Strange, people rarely come to knock on each other's doors here in Brisbane, and I'm not expecting anyone.

When I opened the door to see none other than Ali standing there, I almost fainted in shock. My safe space had just been invaded.

'How did you even know I was here?' I blurted out in my confusion.

He looked demurely down at his feet for a moment, as if for effect. *Don't think I'm going to fall for that act.*

I noticed how impeccably dressed he was as always, in a grey Italian tailored suit with a light shimmer to it this time. *At least he had kept his clothes on today.*

'I got the address from the real estate agent,' came his reply.

'You what?' I repeated in astonishment. 'Why would they just give that out to you? That's my private information.'

'Oh, don't stress Meg,' he said as if he were hushing me like some annoying little child. I was now growing increasingly infuriated.

'And how did you even find them? The estate agents that is.'

'You told me at the time who was managing the property for you and your cousin, remember?' He said, so self-assuredly.

'No, actually. I really don't remember telling you that at all,' I said.

Before I could get the chance to tell him to get lost though, he had already just stepped inside the door, ushered me to the side, and closed it behind him.

You'd think he owned the place.

'I didn't invite you in!'

'I just need a few moments of your day, that's all,' he said with a pleading look in his eyes.

Before I could think, I realised I was already fleeing to the rear of the house, and out the back door. My flight or fight response had kicked in clearly. And I just needed to get as far away from him as possible. I felt trapped and stifled being inside that house with him, and increasingly a little panicked.

Out here in the back yard, I felt a little more free and in control of the awkward and unexpected situation I was finding myself in.

I couldn't even bring myself to speak, so I waited for him to say something.

'I'm really in terrible trouble Meg,' he said wringing his hands together in some pathetic motion which I assume was designed to stir up pity in me. But it didn't. I turned my back to him.

'I know I did a stupid thing Meg,' he continued. 'But you don't understand how much pressure I was being put under in my workplace, and what they've just tried to do to me now. I'm a victim too you see.'

I turned around again to look him in the eye when he said that. He was staring back at me intently, imitating the look of a sad puppy dog needing a mother figure. *Unbelievable.*

'You didn't look like much of a victim to me when you were being entertained by those, erm, professional ladies, on the evening when I saw you last.' My voice was sharp and decisive. I was hoping he would just do the decent thing and leave there and then, but he didn't.

'I know you're upset Meg, and so disappointed in me, just like I am so disappointed in myself. Not just for how I hurt you, but for falling for their trap like that. I know you so well though. I know you're a good person, and when you hear just how much trouble I am in because of them, because of how they tricked me and took advantage of me and the overwhelming situation I felt I was in at work, I know you won't just leave me in this. I really need your help. You are the only person I can turn to right now.'

'What situation are you in?' I asked, almost instantly regretting doing so as soon as I did. *I knew I shouldn't be letting him draw me in, but the truth was, I felt curious to hear what he had to say. Allowing myself to indulge that natural feeling was probably still a mistake in a situation like this however. Afterall, I was dealing with such a rat.*

He crouched down and touched his brow effecting a look of shame and sorrow before he began explaining: 'When I did that awful thing in the hotel with those women, you weren't the only one who saw me doing something shameful and wrong. I was filmed during it too. The ones who did that are trying to blackmail me now. They want tens of thousands from me within the next two months, or they're threatening to have me jailed.'

I was gobsmacked. 'Jailed for what?' I asked.

'It turns out one of the women involved may have been a human trafficking victim that was smuggled in from Asia. They say she will testify that she told me that from the outset. She didn't. I want you to know that I really didn't know. I honestly believed they were both legitimately working as sex providers. The reality is though, especially if I have no-one to support me through this and back me up, I could actually be jailed for having involvement in exploiting her. I could seriously face prison for that Meg. I know you wouldn't want that for me.'

Then he paused and turned on the most doleful looking eyes that I had ever seen. It was rather nauseating and practised looking to me.

'I know I messed up Meg, and I am like dirt at your feet. I wish I could take it all back, I really do. I allowed myself to get so misled by men and women not worth a fraction of a quality woman like you. But please, don't just turn your back on me right now. I need you, and I know that deep down you don't want to leave me alone in this type of trouble. You're a good person Meg. I know you won't just walk away from this.'

I stared at him blankly, realising just how badly he had underestimated my hate filled resolve towards him after what he had done to me. But I said nothing, so he started blabbing on again.

'I just want to know Meg, would you testify for me?'

I kept my silence to let him stew longer in his juices. I was almost beginning to feel slightly amused by his pathetic sorrowful act.

'I really need you right now,' he went on, looking like he was confused by trying to read into my own expression. I presumed he was scanning me for encouraging signs that I might fall for this nonsense, give in to it, and open a door for him to get back into my life. Then he cast his eyes to the ground as if in deep despair. 'I've been contemplating suicide all this past week,' he said next in a more desperate sort of tone while peeking up at me from under his wrinkled brow seeming a bit less confident that he was having the intended effect on me. 'But I started thinking more and more about you, and how loyal and caring you are, even though I never deserved it. So, I decided to pluck up the courage to come up here and implore you.' Then he finally began rising from his pathetic crouched meant to be apologetic position to stand up again.

He looked utterly pathetic to me.

What he said though had sparked some memories of that night again for me. Memories of the night I just wanted to erase from my mind forever. I could vaguely recall the people I saw in the lift with the Canadian or American accents, and realised that they did look a bit out of place. They definitely weren't with Ali's office, so it could very well have been them he was referring to.

'This really isn't my problem anymore,' I said firmly and proudly. 'You're not part of my life now. If you got yourself into a mess, then you will have to get yourself out of it.'

'You don't understand Meg. I just really need your help. Don't let them destroy me like this, we are both victims of those people. It's because of them I've hurt you so much as well, don't let them win.'

Then I realised that to my utter horror, he had leapt towards me and had me in a tight clutch hold. I felt I could barely breathe and was becoming light-headed. This was all just too much. I managed to struggle out of his grip and take a step back. He threw me one of his most pitiful looks again.

'I'm not looking for you to do anything too difficult here. I have a lawyer now, and all I am asking is for you to meet with them. It could really help save me from this.'

He reached out and placed one of his hands on each of my arms. I was then suddenly conscious of hearing a sound coming from Matt's house across the fence.

'What was that?' I said finding the strength to manage to push Ali's arms off of me.

'It's probably just your neighbours,' he said.

'My neighbours are out of town for the Christmas period,' I said. 'Look, I don't think you are understanding me here,' I was trying to be strong. 'I don't ever want to see or hear from you again. I have no interest in testifying or doing anything whatsoever for you. Now please leave my house.'

He looked surprised, but I could see the anger flashing in his eyes too.

After just standing staring me down for a short time, he finally conceded to my firm resolve and said 'I'm sorry I took up your time today.'

What a pathetic guilt trip attempt. It was not going to work on me.

In a last attempt to sway me, he added some emotional blackmail by saying: 'I just really believed you would be here for me.'

'Goodbye Ali.'

With that, he at long last just walked out of my house. A huge sense of relief came over me.

12:00pm After the incredibly stressful visit with Ali, I had just ploughed on with finishing the splashback tiles. It was the best way to stop my mind falling back into the pit of depression again. At least this was all looking good. I now had modern-look light grey splashback tiles. Nothing outdated, and no need to fork out thousands for a tiler to replace them all. That would have been a messy job.

12:15pm While the first coat of tile paint was completely drying off, I decided to go out and check the front letter box. I figured it worthwhile just in case anyone was trying to reach us directly about anything important, rather than doing so via the estate agents. I was becoming increasingly less impressed with them too as time went on. They had no right to give out my investment property address details to Ali. I would have to speak to them about that at some point. But I guessed it would have to wait until at least a week into the New Year when all of Brisbane comes back to work again following the Christmas shut down.

As I approached our little mailbox by the gate, I could see that the postman had put a few things in there this morning. As I was pulling them out, I somehow managed to shove something back out towards the front of the box causing it to fall to the ground on the outside of the fence.

I let out a sigh. It was just too hot at this time of day in the Brisbane summer to be out for long. Even a few steps out to the front of the property with this sweaty dripping humidity felt like a mammoth effort.

When I opened the gate to go outside though, I found the oddest thing. It was a pretty bunch of flowers that appeared just to have been discarded beside the fence.

I picked them up, and saw that there was no name or card to be found on them anywhere, so it didn't seem like a courier had delivered them. I guessed that if no-one wanted them, then I may as well just bring them inside.

The 23ʳᵈ of December

7:00am Was proud of how early I was rising, and how refreshed I was feeling. Mental health was getting back in check, what a relief.

As I sipped on my first coffee of the day, I took the time to start to sift through a little pile of bills and other items which were sent from the estate agent to Tilly that she had clearly never read. Not that I blame her though. Life is hectic, especially when you work full time and have the kind of enviable social life that she does. I'm sure there were many things she was more inclined to be doing than checking over all of this. Besides, we do pay enough to the agents for them to make sure all is in good order as part of their service.

Quickly ascertained that the costliest items we were getting regularly billed for by them, pertained to pest checks and pest control measures.

9:00am After indulging in some lazy lounging and channel surfing, then showering and dressing for the day, my mind began to turn back to subject of those regular pest control services we had been paying for.

I don't know what possessed me, but I decided to actually go back and take a look at the dates the bills claimed the pest control work had been done, and low and behold, the most recent one related to a day the week before. But I was there that whole day, from dawn to dusk, and no-one else came to the property whatsoever. I quickly found myself picking up the phone and calling the named pest control providers directly, just to double check what caused this apparent mistake.

9:25am Was lying flat on my back in the middle of my bed, staring into space in a state of semi-shock and fighting a newly growing headache. I was still trying to process what I had just learned, which was that the pest control company had no record of ever coming out to our rental property, let alone providing and billing for the regular checks, including the fabricated visit last week, as well as a whole series of treatments and barrier spraying that was meant to have been done in recent times. All of it had certainly been billed for by our letting estate agents though, and taken out of our profits for renting out the home.

Unbelievable. What else was false in all of their so-called service provision?

These people in the real estate business were nothing but criminals in fancy suits.

10:00am Had spent some more time fuming over how much we'd been ripped off by our estate agents. Was glad they would likely be closed for the Christmas break already, because much as it might feel cathartic and satisfying, there was nothing to be gained by calling them up and yelling at them.

I wasn't going to make any rash decisions without agreeing on a course of action with cousin Tilly anyhow. But it was clear we needed to end our relationship with these shady property letting people.

Eventually, I could feel a plan growing in my mind: *maybe we should try letting the property out privately*. That way, there would be no need for traitorous estate agents. It couldn't be that hard, and the place had been empty for a while now, in the so-called professionals' hands. We couldn't do much worse really, could we?

Chapter Ten

The 24th of December

8:00am Arrived at the little rental home of ours to do some final tidying, and to appreciate how well I had spruced the place up. I really had brought it more into the current decade in terms of style. And the house just felt so much cleaner now that there were no marks or stains visible on any of the walls.

Well done me!

And you know, this physical work really did help me get through a mentally challenging time and to safely process all the horror memories of Ali swirling through my head. Filed them all away in the ancient history bin where they belong.

Tilly and I had agreed the night before, that when we got around to seeking new tenants in the New Year, this would be something we'd be doing minus dodgy real estate agents. They'd only been cheating us thus far. It would be far easier to sell it to people now with it looking so refreshed. We really don't need them.

8:30am I glanced out through the front window as I wet dusted the ledges and rims, and low and behold, I could see a man full of swagger entering the gate next door. By the look of his neat little ass which was packed into those tight jeans that are so beloved by Italian stallions, I figured that could be the very same man I saw romping butt naked in their house along with his colleague. It's not that he wasn't alluring in some ways or anything, but surely he could keep it in his pants until he got back to his own home. Wouldn't kill him, would it?

He flicked his very dark black hair cooly as he walked inside. While I watched him do that, a niggling question dawned on me: what was he even doing here as if he were working this close to Christmas? I highly doubt he's actually here for anything official at a time like this. Any of them still in their offices at this time of the year are spending their final days before the public holidays getting boozed up while doing seasonal bonding with their colleagues. And, given what I've seen of that guy, probably rather close skin to skin type bonding I should imagine.

Realised that thinking about this and recalling his ultra-petite, hot sex partner and colleague was triggering my Ali-related PTSD. It was making me feel fat or inadequate when I am no such thing!

OK – switching now to new more helpful train of thought. It will not be sexy little black lingerie numbers composed primarily of what looks like fancy strings that I will be lounging around in on this Christmas day. Rather, it will be cute Christmas or tartan patterned nighties that hug these hips of mine and say, I have room to accommodate you, you are ok, because I am awesome, just as me, simply as I am.

8:33am I glanced out of the other window as I moved on to cleaning that one, and I realised that there was a car parked out there that I'd never seen before. They didn't seem to be too worried about getting a parking ticket either. Maybe that was because they knew the parking inspectors are already on holiday by now.

Soon after, I saw another couple of people show up and enter the gate of the house next door. One was a man in his 50s who was wearing a shirt and formal long trousers in this summer heat. The woman with him was about a similar age and she was rather dumpy and severe looking to me.

8:35am I glanced outside again while pottering around and thought I was seeing things. Two cars full of cops were storming the little house next door!

I rubbed my eyes in case I was seeing things. But this was definitely happening.

Surely it wouldn't just be because that over-sexed estate agent was having a hook up in there again, would it? I mean, it's a bit distasteful given the owners don't know and presumably wouldn't approve, but it's not illegal. I can't imagine they'd send multiple cop cars out just for naughty sex.

8:45am I had ventured out to stand and wait on the porch to see if I could see or hear what was going on. But I couldn't hear a thing, what with the distance between our properties and the noise coming from the road.

It wasn't too long however before they began emerging from the door again with three people in handcuffs! I was stunned. They had the over-sexed real estate agent, and the other two I had seen go in shortly after him, all under arrest.

What on earth could they have done?

There was an even bigger surprise in store still though. Following them out of the door closely behind the officers, was none other than Kane!

What on earth was he doing here?

He wasn't under arrest. Thank Goodness.

He turned around and saw me standing on the porch. Just the briefest of waves from him. Then he went on his way. I couldn't help but feel a little bit disappointed at that. I supposed though that he had to go directly give a police statement or something.

I felt rather wistful watching him walk away. I wished I hadn't just dismissed him like I did the last time we met.

Oh, well. Life goes on. Or that's what I told myself at least.

5:10pm Arrived home after some very last-minute Christmas shopping. I only had Tilly to buy for after all. Not much left of our family now, was there?

As I opened the outside lobby door, bags filled with goodies in hand, I noticed a letter had been pushed half inside our mailbox. I wondered whoever could have done that, because it seemed to be after the usual delivery times. I didn't need my key to open the box to collect it, and too lazy to check out the rest, I just grasped that one and headed upstairs.

5:20pm Shopping well hidden away in bedroom to give me time to wrap Tilly's surprise.

Sat down and opened this evening's come lately mystery letter … it had some nice scrolled handwriting on the front it naming me and Tilly. I didn't think many people would even be aware I was up staying here this month. I was increasingly curious to see who this was from.

As I unfolded the letter inside, I was stunned to see it had been signed by Kane. How did he know where I was living? I tried not to be freaked out by that puzzle because I was aware that my spate of bad experiences recently was beginning to make me paranoid … understandably.

I took the time to read his letter before jumping to any conclusions. Happily, it did satisfy my curiosity by explaining that at Kane's instigation, the police had successfully run a sting operation on the dodgy estate agents who were scamming our neighbours next door. It struck me that what they were doing to our neighbours seemed much like our agents were doing to us. I guessed they must have been linked in a joint bid to sell our patches of land off to a high bidding soulless developer.

Oh my heavens above though. Now, not only was he muscular, hot, fit and well-educated, but Kane was a greed and corruption fighting local hero! And I had just let him go! He had struck up the courage to make the move to kiss me, and I ruined it all. This was just getting too much for me.

Then I read on, and things got even worse in terms of my anxiety ... he explained that he had come by to drop off some flowers to our rental home too, by way of an apology. He must have feared in case he'd made me feel awkward, or had offended me in some way the last time he saw me. Then, he explained, he had seen me with a man whom he assumed was my boyfriend, so he didn't want to disturb me.

I could have blown a gasket there and then. How frustrating. I didn't even know where Kane lived, and he hadn't put his address on the top of his letter either. I might never see him again!

This was all too distressing for me right now. Must distract myself, I decided.

8:30pm Had a fairly distracting viewing of *It's a Wonderful Life* behind me. I felt dreamy and transported back to a younger simpler time of my life. But now I was finding thoughts of Kane drifting back into my mind again already.

8:45pm Made myself get up to wrap Tilly's presents for tomorrow, and placed them under the tree. That gesture always made me feel like a little kid again!

I allowed myself a moment to reflect on my late loved ones. I closed my eyes and imagined they were here still, standing around me. For a moment, when I focused hard enough, I could almost feel their love, feel the warmth, and imagine our arms around one another.

Chapter Eleven

The 25th of December

6:00am Just like a couple of little children, Tilly and I were up with the birds and tearing the wrapping paper off excitedly to see what this Christmas had brought us. Something about us being together for the first time since we actually were youngsters, just brought the whole nostalgia of it all back to us both. I missed those old days, though while I was in them, all I wanted to do more than anything else, was to grow up as quickly as possible.

One quick tear and cousin Tilly's present was unveiled. I was not disappointed: it was Madonna, Celebration, the video collection from the 80s itself, but on DVD!!!! How awesome.

I felt tears of laughter come to my eyes. 'Remember how much fun we used to have dancing to all of those?'

'Well, of course, that's precisely why I thought this would be the perfect gift. Even when you head back down to Sydney, you can put this on and remember our Christmas here together too.'

'Thank you, Tilly,' I said, while reaching over to hug her.

'My favourite was definitely *Material Girl*. Do you remember the time I made cones like the Madonna bra and got into so much trouble from Gran who was affronted?!'

'Yes, I do remember that,' said Tilly smiling. 'That is just so typically you.'

'I remember at a young age thinking how sensible her advice was in that song, but I fear that I have already totally failed in the more feminist plan to live my life like that. I'm sitting here now with nothing to show for my life really,' I sighed a bit. 'I made absolutely nothing out of any relationship I ever had with any man, and of course, they all just walk away when they're done with you.'

'Well, you know what?' said Tilly with her straight face on.

'What?' I said, still enjoying my self-pity party rather too much.

'At least you tried!'

That did make me laugh at least.

10am Arrived at the beach with our picnic baskets in hand. Tilly was wearing the new pair of designer sunnies I got her for Christmas. I had shelled out a bit more for a particularly nice gift to say thanks to her for letting me stay for a few weeks the way she had.

As I looked around me at everyone having fun by the water, I was so reminded of older times I almost became overwhelmed. I felt a bit of a lump starting in my throat. It took a moment until the almost unbearable urge to reminisce had passed. I always did find that experiencing memories of the past was tinged with rather too much sorrow over the knowledge that days gone by can never be relieved. It was meant to be bitter sweet though, as people say, when you reflect on the by gone days. But, I think I am just more comfortable with the sweeter side of life wherever possible.

The Goldie hadn't changed too much since I moved Sydney side. It was still full of half-naked bodies and families everywhere. It was nice to be amongst this on such a happy day of the year though, because the energy I felt all around me was simple. It was just about relaxing, chilling, and having some fun.

So, I lathered on the sunscreen and ran into the ocean. Pure cool bliss on such a searingly hot day!

10:35am Tilly and I set about setting up our little beach shade tent as per the modern trends. As true Queenslanders though, it almost felt to me like we were betraying some unwritten code. We never did this when we were growing up here. Our beaches had never looked at all like the ones in Europe did during the high season, what with their umbrellas, shades, and even deck chairs everywhere! But the truth was, it made good old-fashioned sense to have one of these shade structure things.

10:58am Was drying off still in the pleasant shade of my tent and reading a book, when I saw an incredibly muscly man start playing ball in front of me (with his equally buff mates). I wondered for a moment if I was looking at a team of our professional rugby players or something, but honestly, I wouldn't even be able to pick then out in a crowd.

'Are you seeing this too Tilly?' I asked her. 'Don't you think they are real professional sportsmen or something?'

'Maybe they are, for all I would know,' she replied.

Then, next thing I knew, I was rubbing my head realising I had been hit by a stray volley ball.

'Was it one of the rugby team?' I heard myself asking. Tilly was hovering over me with a distressed look. I realised at that point that was because I had sort of toppled over on to my side by this stage. I think I was seeing floaters.

'I am so sorry,' I heard a man say as he stuck his dark hair draped face right over mine.

'Please stop,' I said in urgency, 'I don't need CPR or anything, I'm totally fine.'

I levelled my body back up straight. 'Are you one of the professional players?' I asked.

'No, I'm not,' said the man who I assume had thrown the ball that struck me. He looked bemused. 'I'm just an amateur ball player, as you can probably tell by now.'

'Oh, you're too funny,' Tilly was saying in a rather flirty way. In fact, she definitely was making her sheep eyes at that guy, oh my. I felt like a third wheel already.

'I'm fine, I'm fine,' I reassured everyone.

Then a group of other young men came over.

'Anyone up to try turning the barbie on yet?' asked Tilly.

'They're probably all taken by now,' I said. But I knew we had optimistically packed some meat and other goodies in ice, just in case we could get hold of one.

'We do actually have one already,' said the man who hit me with a ball, 'you'd be welcome to share it with us, and in fact, it's the least we could do given how I just hit you like that.'

'That would be great,' said Tilly eagerly and before I could even get a word in.

'OK,' he said, beginning to look at her with equally sheepish eyes and a queasy smile. 'Just come over and we can get you set up. I'll show you where it is.'

As we followed him and made our way over to their spot, we found out there were about 20 in his group.

'There's a huge bunch of you,' said Tilly. 'Are you all family?'

'Oh no,' he said, then went on to explain that he was here with a bunch of work colleagues. Everyone here worked in the same research centre as him and it was a very international mix of people they had come along with.

12:00 Noon By now, the barbie was well underway. A few trays had been served onto plates and put aside to keep warm. Would not be long until the feast was ready. We had chucked our plates in along with everyone else's in very true traditional Aussie style.

I sipped my sparkling wine some more while continuing to make small talk with friends of the man I now knew as Adam, rather than just that dark haired guy who hit me on the head with a ball earlier.

I glanced over my shoulder and saw that he and Tilly were still engrossed in each other's conversation. They were sitting a little bit away from the rest of our group on a neat patch of grass nearby. Looked to me like those two had really hit it off. *Would be nice if Tilly got someone in her life*, I thought, but watching them together brought thoughts of Kane back to my mind, and that made me feel rather sad. I had to learn to get better at not linking unrelated things in life together in my head like that. For it meant that any bad experience in one thing in my life can taint others that are going perfectly well. When I get more control over negative thought linking like that, I will be much happier day to day. Or so my therapist keeps trying to teach me at least. One day I will get there.

12:45pm I was feeling totally stuffed, and a little tipsy, but completely happy and at peace with myself. Looking at the beautiful subtropical paradise I was born in, I couldn't help but feel a true sense of gratitude. I really should try to appreciate all of this much more than I have done.

Then, all in an instant, my inner peace was gone. It was Ali. He was here, standing right in front of me, on my beach, on my Christmas Day interrupting this precious time I was having with my only close family left.

How did he even know I was here?

I felt my blood beginning to boil. I saw that Tilly had cottoned on to what was happening and she was making her way over to me. She put an arm on my shoulder. The support was very welcome, and it felt good. For once I wasn't just dealing with someone treating me badly and trying to emotionally blackmail me further all on my own. Because big girls really do cry sometimes.

'Hi Meg,' he called over. *Sickeningly smarmy as always. Oh how I wish that aspect of his character had irritated me back when I first met him.*

'And Tilly, oh Merry Christmas to you both,' he said reaching out as if he was going to try to hug me. I took a step back at that and looked away awkwardly. He got the message.

'I won't take up too much of your time on this lovely day,' he continued, trying to guilt trip me from the outset. At least I understood that he was manipulating me like that now and there was no way I was falling for any of it. I would not be having a bar of it, as Dad used to say.

'I just really need to talk to you,' he went on.

'How did you even know where we were today?' I interrupted with.

'Someone told me you'd be here,' he said with a straight face.

'Someone told you I would be here?' I repeated incredulously. I looked at Tilly who looked similarly bewildered.

'Frankly, this is just getting weird and stalkerish now,' I said with impatience.

'No, it's really not,' he said. 'If you just come over to the side with me for a moment, I'll explain to you what's been going on.'

He put his hands on my arm and tried to gently pull me. I started resisting, then before I knew what was happening or could open my mouth to tell him to get off me, he fell to the ground having been smacked in the side of the face.

The man who had just hit him looked to be 50 at least, and he was still stroking his fist in fiery rage. His face burned red with his anger. He looked so weak and wispy with little tails of grey hair in tufts around his head, but my, my, he sure packed a punch.

My God, what brought this on him? Surely this wasn't just someone trying to defend my honour because my arm was being pulled a bit.

Then I found out.

'You took our entire life savings. My wife passed away yesterday, and we had nothing at the end,' he yelled at Ali. 'In our last year together, we should have been travelling around Australia like we'd planned. We would have been able to if you hadn't conned me. You convinced me of how I could make such a great nest egg using my self-managed super funds. You told me that I could leave my children something to be proud of, and all with your help and guarantees.'

A crowd had gathered around us by this point, and many were cheering the angry older man on. Some were calling the police about it.

I can't say I was sorry to see Ali floored like that. I wanted him out of my life for good too. Looking down at him though, I just felt so above it all, and so much stronger now.

Then I noticed that someone seemed to be pushing through the crowd and it seemed like the police were here already.

It was Kane! This was the best Christmas present a girl like me could wish for. I had been pining over him all day.

'This is him, this is your man,' Kane was saying to the officers, and the next thing I knew, they were reading Ali his rights and placing him under arrest.

Kane's eyes caught mine, he smiled an acknowledging greeting in my direction, but still looked rather serious.

I was so overwhelmed that for the first time in my life I understood the cartoonlike swoon some people do at moments like this. I managed to remain composed and standing though. And there was no sign of Miss Baywatch being with Kane today either, fabulous.

After exchanging some words with the police, Kane made his way towards me.

I saw Ali shoot an angry look in my direction as they took him away. I didn't move a single face muscle to react. I was just glad when he was gone again.

'I hope he wasn't bothering you too much before I got here,' said Kane, 'I mean, I completely understand that you might've wanted to spend some more time with him again today.' Then he started awkwardly looking down at his feet.

I felt so confused, so I blurted out, 'Oh, not at all, you've got the wrong end of the stick there. I don't want to see that man ever again.'

'Really?' he said as though he didn't believe me.

'Yes, really,' I said back. 'Why would you think that though?' *Decided I was just going to ask him, sod me running the unanswered questions over and over in my mind for the rest of the night.* But then I almost instantly realised that I probably already knew the answer. Before he had a chance to explain I asked 'Was it because you saw him at the rental home when you came to drop off some flowers?'

'Well, yes, that was why actually. I just happened to see that he was there so I assumed you were together, you know, as in a couple. I hadn't told you this yet of course, but as you have seen now, I was already on to that man too. I suspected long ago that he was a big part of that ring targeting the land in the area your investment home is on. And of course I was right. Hopefully through him the names of more money launderers will come out in the wash.'

My heart sank. I don't quite know why this hurt me so much. Even after all the betrayal I had already learned of and processed that had involved that man, this really took the wind out of my sails. I felt like my mind was turning over and starting to question absolutely everything, like nothing could be trusted now. It sounded like some great big conspiracy theory from someone in the grip of a mental health crisis, but it was really the truth. I had just seen it with my own eyes. The police had actually come and arrested him just like they did with the estate agents next door. *Stupid old me.*

'Look, I'm really sorry I had to tell you that,' said Kane, and he looked like he meant it. 'It's never easy for anyone to find out they've been conned like this. From what I found out when I was investigating these people, it seems to me that Ali actually picked you out and went after you. That was from the point at which he first learned that you were soon to inherit that rental property of your grandparents.'

The hurt was becoming physical now. I actually felt a sharp pain go through my heart, then I started to feel like I might vomit. I tried to recall my therapists' advice for times like these which was to take a big breath and try to come back into the present moment. I gently closed my eyes as I did so, then when I opened them again I was struck with the beauty of Kane's eyes that were looking deeply into mine and had moved a little closer.

'Are you ok?' he asked.

I felt Tilly rubbing my back in sympathy.

'Yes, I'll be fine,' I half laughed and half cried.

'I'm really sorry,' Kane said again.

Then I did the most spontaneous thing I had done in as long as I can remember. I threw my arms around Kane and kissed him directly on the lips. To my great relief he kissed me back.

I had made it home for Christmas alright. This was the most sensuous, warm and connected I had felt to anything for such a long time. *I am me, exactly where I'm meant to be, and I'm loving it!*

Chapter Twelve

Boxing day the 26ᵗʰ of December

9:20am I opened my eyes to see Kane lying beside me in my bed. To say things had gone well since Ali's arrest yesterday would be an understatement. For the briefest of moments, I had feared in case I had just dreamt the night before, but it was real.

The way we had talked and laughed so much together yesterday on that special day of the year was magical. Kane was full of bright ideas to make things better going forward for landlords and all residents in our local area too. He had suggested that landlords like us get together and form a collective to help support one another in private letting, with no dodgy oversexed estate agents involved. We could also become a powerful force to lobby together for more responsible and well thought out development in our rapidly growing beloved city of Brisbane.

That wasn't his only bright idea though. It seemed I was more on his mind than I could ever have imagined these past couple of weeks. He had asked me if I would like him to have a word to a friend of his who was in my line of work. If there might be a role for me up here, I wouldn't have to go back down to Sydney. And you know, I realised I didn't have much to go back down for anyhow. That coupled with Kane now shaping up to be a big part of my life meant that staying home in Brisbane for the foreseeable future was what my heart was guiding me to do.

Yesterday evening had just been about togetherness. Having Kane come back to Tilly's was just like having a third family member. It felt natural, it felt easy, it felt right. It was nice to have fallen asleep next to a man who wasn't pressuring me in any way. Enjoyed closeness, but no sex … well, just yet! We were taking things slowly, we would get to know each other, and hopefully we would never look back.

Home for Christmas
©2025 Dr Clare Anne McGrory.
All Rights Reserved Worldwide.